A Sense
of the
Midlands

A Sense *of the* Midlands

Edited by Cynthia Boiter

Poetry editor ~ Ed Madden

A SENSE OF THE MIDLANDS.

Copyright 2014 by Cynthia Boiter. All rights reserved.

Printed in the United States of America. No part of this book may be used or produced in any manner whatsoever without written permission except in the case of brief quotations embodied in critical articles and reviews. For information address Muddy Ford Press, 1009 Muddy Ford Road, Chapin, South Carolina, 29036.

Library of Congress Number: 2014932442

ISBN: 978-0-9838544-8-7

Cover art by Jarid Lyfe Brown

"I can, with one eye squinted, take it all as a blessing."

Flannery O'Connor

Contents

Preface 1

Heart of the Heartland – Tom Poland 3

Sight

Dirt – Dianne Turgeon Richardson 11

Reclaiming the Track – Melanie Griffin 13

The Vernacular of Disaster – James Barilla 15

Under the Rainbow of the Chicken Man 29
 – Thomas Maluck

Before the Divorce – Julie Bloemeke 31

US-321—circle you are subtle – Zach Mueller 33

Tiny Predators – Darien Cavanaugh 35

The Delta – Matthew Boedy 37

Neighbors – Nicola Waldron 47

Manifest Destiny – Dianne Turgeon Richardson 49

Sound

You stay in Columbia or are forgotten with Adluh Flour 53
— Brandi L. Perry

When We Stopped Talking about the Weather 55
— Ray McManus

The Mare – Ivan Young 57

Neighbor – Lauren Allen 59

Riff – Kevin Simmonds 61

Music and Dancing atop Arsenal Hill 63
— Kristine Hartvigsen

Shandon – Nan Ancrom 67

Kayak Journal – Randy Spencer 69

What the Moon Say – Robbie Pruitt 73

Neighbor – Ed Madden 75

A Brief History of Bowling – Laurel Blossom 77

Excerpt from *South: A Memoir* – Nicola Waldron 79

Close to Nature – Ruth Varner 85

Saturday Morning – Ray McManus 89

The Bats – Ivan Young 91

Possum – Ed Madden 93

Southern Lit after 1900 – Brandi L. Perry 95

Touch

Fishing with Dad – Jennifer Bartell 99

Pilgrimage – Lauren Allen 101

Autumn Angels – Rieppe Moore 103

The Gardener – Alexis Stratton 105

Taste

Cantaloupe – Melissa Johnson 111

Dreher Island Produce – Terresa Haskew 113

'Que – Frank Thompson 115

Independence Day – Ed Madden 119

Worship at Lake Murray – Terresa Haskew 123

Forbidden Fruit – Melissa Johnson 125

Smell

Chinese Snowball Viburnum – Melissa Johnson 129

As I Look Back – Mahayla Bainter 131

Your confession on the pontoon near Jake's Landing 133
– Linda Lee Harper

When Dawn Comes – Cassie Premo Steele 135

Salt Atlas – Matthew Fogarty 157

Preface

My favorite sense is smell. It's not the sense that I would choose to keep, if I had to choose only one and, in fact, it would be one of the first I'd give away if the choice were forced upon me. Certainly not sight, sound, or touch. I can't imagine going without seeing the faces of the people I love, or hearing their voices and feeling their embraces. But truth be told, there are any number of smells I could go without ever sniffing again—bad tomatoes, cat litter, and chain smokers, to name a few.

Still, there's something about the grounding qualities of smell that is both lasting and transporting, particularly to the Southern nose. The smell of burgers on the grill, for example, takes me to Williams-Brice Stadium as aromas from the hardcore tailgating tents waft into the stands above. The amalgamated smell of French fries and funnel cake takes me back down to those same fairgrounds where every sense is over-stimulated in a fury. When I smell hot tar I become my seven-year-old self playing in the deserted middle of a summer's tar-and-gravel country road, dreaming of going as far away as it would take me. Fresh cut watermelon, however, and I'm that same young girl, but perfectly content at a picnic table in my family's big backyard. Smells, and the memories with which they are loaded, can be unpredictable.

Everyone has a favorite sense; and by favorite I mean magical. A sight or sound or stroke of the breeze that sends us instantaneously to a place of wistfulness or yearning. For Dianne Turgeon Richardson, it is the gritty touch of sand in her shoes from the shores of Lake Murray. It is sight that resonates with Darien Cavanaugh as he writes about the "hard beauty" of night hawks weaving "in long, slow arcs" alongside the monument to slavery on the South Carolina statehouse grounds. And, for Terresa Haskew, there is reverence in the taste of a Bloody Mary, sipped from a Solo cup on a drowsy Sunday morning; nothing short of a religious experience. Like miraculous superpowers, our senses and their stored memories can move us through time and space to places both fictional and all-too-real.

All of the experiences recorded in this anthology are grounded in the unique and ever-present sensations that accompany life in the South Carolina Midlands. The poems, essays, excerpts, and bits of short fiction that follow come from a shared sense of place. What we have seen, smelled, tasted, touched, and heard are the things that make us Midlanders. As Flannery suggested, take it all as a blessing.

Cynthia Boiter

February 2014

Heart of the Heartland

By Tom Poland

Naïve, unsure, and lost in more ways than I could count, I first came to the Midlands in 1971. A 100-mile drive down Highway 378 from a three-light town in Georgia brought me to West Columbia one autumn evening. The sun had set and across a river stood Paris. City lights danced across a rock-studded Congaree as I drove over a bridge evocative of Europe. The Gervais Street Bridge's arches and lights convinced me I was entering the City of Lights.

A country boy had done come to town.

I spent two days seeing the city and two nights sleeping in a bay window on Senate Street. It felt Parisian. Two years later, windblown like some fern spore, I landed here and began to seek my writer's voice. Sensory experiences—good and bad—would mold that voice here in the Midlands.

"Midlands." It sounds too much like "middling," something average. I prefer Heartland. Trapped between the smoky blue Upcountry and marshy, green Lowcountry, the Heartland gets overlooked but it flaunts an emerald crown jewel known as Congaree National Park. There the interplay of sunlight and water sustains the country's largest surviving contiguous tract of old-growth bottomland hardwoods. I appreciate things that quietly endure as we people wrapped up in our noisy day-to-day lives come and go into that dark, dark night. Congaree is such a place. Congaree teaches patience, something writers understand. The later years bring rewards but for now you must be resolute and resourceful.

Here in the Heartland I found treasures. Come. I'll show you what I mean. Let's walk over to a Lexington County peach orchard. Treading ancient dunes we see the blossoms' fine pink blush, delicate like a young woman's lips. In bright July light we'll inhale the intoxicating fragrance of ripe peaches, a bouquet suggestive of things sweeter than kisses. Eat a peach. Taste the Heartland.

Stroll through a country garden and pluck jewels that delight the eye and taste—tomatoes, cucumbers, and yellow crookneck squash. Near St. Matthews summer wheat puts off such a fresh, sweet fragrance you'll swear you're in a bakery, and you are—the sun's kitchen.

Though the coast is far away, crab cakes, shrimp and grits ain't. Restaurants bring gems inland from the sea. What's more southern than a pat of butter melting in grits clean crushed between ancient millstones. Boykin Mill rolls on, preserving the days when mills provided fresh cornmeal, grits, and flour. Plunge your hand into freshly milled flour. It's warm, warmth Old Sol FedExed here expressly for you.

If old Granby Ferry is famously hot, the Heartland is famously photogenic. Portraits abound. In early darkness my confederate, a photographer, stalks dawn. Soon a gossamer veil of light falls upon Saluda River rapids. Soft clicks capture it. Lit up, the river sings its river song. Along its banks ferns bunched like collards green up. Their moist fern spores smell like crushed spices, and humus releases its earthy, rich, uplifting fragrance, the scent of life rising from death. Across the river in Elmwood Cemetery, scents of death drift about. The Broad River purls beneath the bluff where Confederate soldiers sleep, but it's the recently departed who give Elmwood its verboten scent on sizzling summer days. Generous winds, however, and a sweeping Heartland sky serve up favors.

Come cooler months fleecy cirrus clouds stretch into streamers that splatter color across the sky. Daylight dies a beautiful death when a cold front brings meteorological theatrics to town. Winter sunsets over Lake Murray and Wateree are not to be missed.

Up near Blythewood a plume of fragrant woodsmoke floats up. Something about smoke pouring from a chimney speaks of departed grandparents and old smokehouses. Sugar-cured hams and brewing coffee come to mind. Roaring fireplaces too.

In fall we stack sour-smelling split oak as children dream of snow but it seldom comes. Spring, however, fetches blizzards. We love spring's dogwoods but fear her squalls. Lightning unleashes the acrid smell of ozone and fires. March winds topple trees and whitecaps march across lakes. I would be remiss by the way if I didn't devote a few more lines to water. At the confluence of the Broad and Saluda, diminishing rocky shoals spider lilies cling to rocks. It's a damn shame we love dams, lakes, and hydroelectric power as much as we do.

"Water, water, everywhere ..." Drive down I-26 toward Charleston and you'll see H.G. Wells's Martian invaders from *The War of the Worlds*. Like alien craft center-pivot irrigation systems conquer dust and dryness with whirling jets of water. In Wells's book red weed spread wherever water ran; in the Heartland green crops sprout and run thick all the way to market.

Flora aplenty here. At the Governor's Mansion yellow roses twine around Doric columns, giving off a sweet fragrance counterpoint to the dry metallic scent of wrought iron gates—poetry forged from glimmering yellow-red lines struck by yesteryear's master lyricist, the blacksmith. Listen hard and hear his hammer clang.

A handsome past hides here. Sepia toned by dust and time, old country stores stand empty, reminders of days when men in suspenders and felt hats operated charming centers of commerce. Run your fingers through the dust on an old store's countertop. Like pollen, it clings to the fingertips, but unlike pollen it cannot reproduce itself. Gone for good, an illusion at best.

Seeing isn't always believing. Mirages writhe like snakes along blistering Heartland highways but you won't find any on an old Spanish moss-oak-shaded road in the High Hills of Santee. You will see historic sites and feel you're in the mountains and coast all at once. It's a curious sight to see Spanish moss in mountain-like terrain but that's what Highway 261 gives you. State Route 261 winds through an area that's rural, isolated, and heartbreakingly antebellum. Ruins dwell here but I've yet to find them. I find them elsewhere. The columned ruins of Millwood Plantation and Saluda Factory's stone keystone arch impress and depress. In one fell swoop you see that, yes, someone had a dream and the dream was realized but its fate was to end in utter disaster. Ruins speak to us. "Take heed. Here is where grand ideas and mighty events came to pass, but not so mighty as to prevent our destruction."

Music, like ruins, speaks to us. One night fiddles inspired by Appalachia wandered out of a West Columbia pickin' parlor into my soul. For some reason I thought of the nearby Congaree River. Then I thought of the Gervais Street Bridge. That bridge changed my life. That bridge ferried me back to a bay window on Senate Street. That bridge and a bay window charted my path. They opened a way and a window to the world, a world of joys with dashes of sadness and disappointment thrown in for good measure. Grounding balance you could say.

Once upon a time a country boy landed in the not-so-middling region between the smoky blue Upcountry and marshy, green Lowcountry and saw what to him was Paris. He liked what he saw and in time found not just his voice. He found himself in a place people call the Midlands, a place he calls the Heartland.

Sight

Dirt

By Dianne Turgeon Richardson

Sandhills

The Carolina of my childhood is sand,
an inland beach of struggling pines,
grit in my shoes whenever I played outside,
clear-cut, graded parcels of scrub oak land
where vinyl siding and Bradford pears would go,
Taco Bells and traffic lights and fluorescent glow
and a shopping center where pecans once grew.

Red Clay

There was no red clay in my childhood.
It existed on the other side of the river
where my father lived with his wife,
where my stepbrothers rode four-wheelers,
played baseball and sang Baptist hymns,
where Lake Murray sweeps the dirt down to bedrock
and the Saluda leaves a red smudge in every backyard
when it rains.

Reclaiming the Track

By Melanie Griffin

Never did run in high school
But now we do.
Not away, or to, but around—
Around and around and around.
We put our days in the middle.
We hide them in the grass
Or on the tar—in the dark layers
Of a suburban Saturday night.
We spring off the asphalt
To marvel at the cool air
To drag it through our lungs
To catch glimpses and winks of porch lights—
Just beyond our fringes.
We circle our days
Until they are the right size
And we fall down sweating beside them
Watching the headlights and stars
Push their ways through

The Vernacular of Disaster

By James Barilla

First, it's a storm watch. Every television station has its own graphic ready to deploy. Hundreds of miles to the west, there are reports of tornadoes, and the weather people are on the lookout as the system tracks toward North Carolina.

We're not watching the skies, however. We're having a barbeque at my sister's house in the suburbs of Raleigh. Cousins are chasing each other around the yard under the indulgent supervision of grandparents. Hopeful dogs are watching parents plate up lunch by the grill. There's nothing prophetic above us, just a wisp of cirrus here, a clot of stratus there, drifting in a warm blue haze.

We sit in the sunshine and wait.

Hurricanelandia

I've spent much of my life learning the vernacular of place: the local flora and fauna, foods, building materials, soil qualities, human cultures, the folklore that grows up around what's useful. You have to go out looking for these things. Recently I've come to realize, however, that disaster is also part of the lexicon. You don't find it, necessarily. It finds you.

The signs of local calamity, the way the sky behaves, the longstanding patterns of human anticipation, the behavior of birds and livestock: these are regionally distinctive. But it's also true, in this era of accelerating climate change, that your local language of environmental catastrophe and mine, your flood and my drought, are connected in ways they've never been before. The vernacular of place is evolving, a sign that what it means to dwell in a place is undergoing a subtle transformation. Contemporary disasters divide us into regions, and unify us at the same time.

My family has recently moved to Columbia, South Carolina, on the interior edge of what Philip Gerard once called *Hurricanelandia*. This is my first time living in the South, and I've been learning about the geography of our tropical cyclone basin, how the islands descend from Florida like vertebrae, the continent's bony tail. How a storm seems to vacillate, prevaricate, turning one way and then the other, unsure. Will it come for us on the Eastern Seaboard? Or head for the Gulf Coast, for New Orleans or Galveston? The computer models splay out potential tracks, proliferating, some harmless, some devastating.

Our house is a hundred miles inland, but I've been warned of the potential for storms to come ashore, veer west, and roar up the Santee River basin to Columbia. It's happened before, a sudden crook in the cyclonic finger tracing the shore, as if these personified convections of water and air were capable of whimsy.

Skywatching

At my sister's house, the tornado warning has been issued. The roll call of communities in harm's way scrolls across the bottom of the television screen while pitcher faces batter in a sunny baseball stadium somewhere far away. My brother-in-law opens his laptop and brings up the radar. To the south of our municipal dot, we see a roiling mass of neon reds and yellows and purples, color combinations that in nature often signal something deadly, a poison dart frog, bright as a gemstone and glistening with alkaloid toxins. *Heed my warning*, those colors say, *or I'll sizzle your heart, make your limbs dangle.*

Outside, it's hazy. A few droplets have left dark stains on the sidewalk, but otherwise the air is thick and warm and still, like a long-held breath. The kids are inside now, playing upstairs. My instinct is to buckle them into their car seats and get on the road. But where would we go? Where are we safer than right here in the driveway? I feel disoriented, unprepared. We've moved from the Upper Midwest, where the risk of funnel clouds was real enough that our town installed warning sirens. But those sirens never sounded; the reliable menace was snow. That's what I'm programmed for: lake effect, school closure, salt and snow plow. I learned the unwritten code of the Blizzard Belt. Don't go anywhere. Hunker down. Bundle up and hope the heat stays on, the lights don't flicker out.

In hurricane country, the official advice is to flee. Get out while the getting's good. South Carolina coastal communities have evacuation plans, blue signs with whirling white cyclone symbols marking escape routes from the islands. The hurricane watch allows us time to assess risk. I used to think of bioregional identity as a celebration of place: the unique interplay of nature and culture, biogeography and community spirit. But perhaps its most intuitive expression lies in risk assessment. As long as there have been humans here, they have been scanning the horizon, figuring out where and when to take shelter.

Last hurricane season, none of my neighbors paid much attention to the storm watches. They knew better. *We were the Midlands*, pine forests and rolling hills; *we were not the Lowcountry*, the moss-draped and brooding Carolina coast. We had learned to assume a bioregional identity by watching news reports. With a storm on the horizon, we no longer thought of ourselves as residents of cities and towns; we were from barrier islands and river basins, coastal swamps and foothills. All of us needed to know the particulars of our location. Some could rest easy. Others had to be on alert.

Now we watch the sky from my sister's backyard. I wonder: Does risk assessment apply to funnel clouds? "Tornado Alley" is the colloquial expression for the broad swath of the central United States where the risk is greatest— Kansas, Oklahoma, Nebraska, Texas—but it's a misleading term. Funnel clouds of varying intensities occur regularly even in Alaska. Raleigh isn't traditionally included in the Tornado Alley riskscape, and yet here we are, faces turned upward, with trouble on the horizon.

What are we watching for? An eerie green tint to the sky? Crows behaving strangely? Toads falling out of the sky? The kids are still playing in the yard; the neighbor is mowing his grass. How will we speak of the storm when it touches down? Our hurricanes are personified with human names, but tornadoes are too numerous to name, too localized, too ephemeral to share. They are labeled with the Enhanced Fujita Scale, which measures the potential for wind damage, but an "EF-5 tornado" doesn't fix the event in place or time or lend itself to story. When it comes to twisters, there is no Katrina, no Camille, no Andrew.

Sailor Take Warning

A few months earlier, I'd gone to see Cary Mock, a paleoclimatologist who uses ship's logs, plantation diaries and newspaper accounts of the days before satellite images to reconstruct a meteorological history of the region. Mock is a walking compendium of disaster folklore — he can describe the worst hurricane in Carolina history with details gleaned from the meticulous notes of a 17th-century weather nut, or name the town that's had the worst luck dodging storms (McClellanville, north of Charleston). If anyone has a sense of place that looks less like a postcard and more like a bioregional riskscape, it would be him.

We met in a room near his office where leather tomes shared space with stacks of scrolled maps. I half-expected a salty dog of the sea to appear, but Mock looks nothing like a blustering sea captain. He has thickish glasses, black hair that falls across his field of vision, the hyped up air of a storm chaser. Never mind that the storms he tracks are hundreds of years old.

I was hoping he might help me understand something I'd observed in my neighbors, who often looked at the sky and felt the wind against their faces. What did they see there? Was it just me, or did the weather coming from the tropics almost taste of those latitudes, like something steeped in mangroves and the musk of sugarcane fields? Could we smell the dust of distant feedlots in the dry western winds? What did a hurricane smell like? I thought Mock's research might hold the key to the vernacular of disaster, a regional refinement of the old adage, "Red skies at night, sailor's delight; red skies in the morning, sailor take warning."

It turns out, however, that folk history doesn't offer coastal residents much when it comes to predicting individual storms. While some ship captains had barometers to help them detect an approaching weather event, most land dwellers didn't have such tools. Plantation diaries do contain observations of ominous shifts in the tides and references to the phases of the moon, but those often produced false positives. Until the arrival of the telegraph at the end of the 19th century, coastal residents usually had no warning of an oncoming hurricane. They simply had to survive it. In other words, their experience was pretty similar to the contemporary experience of a tornado.

There are accounts, gathered from the residents of Sea

Island, of what it was like to live through a massive hurricane that swept over that spit of sand in 1893. No radar gave warning when the storm arrived in the middle of the night — these people heard the wind clawing away the roof of their dwellings, and soon they felt water rising beneath their beds as the storm surge washed over the island. Many recalled the terror of the darkness they endured, a primeval darkness that left them not only helpless but blind.

That was a storm with no name. It is called, simply, the 1893 Sea Island hurricane. The practice of assigning human names to tropical storms is a more recent development, beginning after World War II with the advent of improved meteorology. We named the storms because we could track them; they were no longer a disaster we had to blindly survive but a phenomenon we could characterize. In this way, the bioregional riskscape evolved in response to technological advances. The vernacular assimilated these new ways of envisioning our place in the world.

Shelter in Place

Now it's decision time. All scheduled programming has been preempted, and the news reporters, their voices trilling with adrenaline, are toggling between images of the whirling tornadoes and the seething vat of the Doppler. They've zoomed in to the neighborhood level now, and they've overlaid the blotchy radar with violet parallelograms of anxiety.

"If you are in this area," they warn, tracing the area just north of downtown with a pointer, "you should seek shelter immediately. Again we repeat, this is a very serious storm coming through your area. Take shelter immediately in a basement if possible. If you don't have a basement, go to an interior room in the house and wait for the all clear."

Is this actually happening? Am I actually looking toward the downstairs bathroom and wondering how many of us could fit in there? We're north of downtown, maybe a bit east of where they're pointing, but what does that mean? Are we far enough away? I want to jump in the car and haul ass out of there, but of course you can't do that with a twister. There is no tornado evacuation route. We're stuck here, sheltering in place.

All twelve of us are in front of the television now, nervously trying to assimilate the information and assess the threat. All except my brother-in-law, who's tracking a different radar projection on his laptop. "We're here," he says, pointing to an area just north of one of the freeways that ring the city. He runs his finger down from the red boil covering the house to where a crescent of lilac and magenta curves back toward itself. "That hook is where the danger is," he says. "That's the leading edge."

How does he know this? He's not a storm chaser or a weather nut. In the background, I can hear the announcers ratcheting up through the octaves of hysteria. "People in these areas of North Raleigh should take shelter immediately. This storm will be moving through your area in the next five minutes. We repeat …"

Five minutes? That's our warning? No wonder there's no prophetic vernacular for tornadoes — there's no time for it to develop. What should we do? It's not even windy outside yet, but they're showing scary scenes from downtown, and that's what, a 10-minute drive at most?

"Maybe we should think about heading to the basement," I suggest.

"Nah," my brother-in-law says, settling into the couch. "It's not coming through here. It's south of us. We haven't even lost power yet."

He's right about that; we still have the wireless modem and the cable connection, still have our climate-controlled interior that makes us feel insulated from the vagaries of the weather. But as he finishes speaking, the wind rises suddenly, buffeting the treetops with a sound like someone yanking aside a curtain. Just as suddenly the rain comes down, a thousand nails clattering onto the roof all at once. The gutters start gushing water. The lights flicker.

The wind itself is strange; the treetops are being tossed back-and-forth in a frenzy, but there's nothing but a quiet eddy below. Three minutes away now? It feels, on some tingling somatic level, like something's coming.

"I think we're going under the house," I announce, reaching for my daughter's arm.

"Right now."

The basement is little more than a crawlspace cut into the slope of the yard. To get to it, we have to dash across the backyard to the door, which happens to be right underneath a gushing torrent of run-off from the roof. One by one, all twelve of us, aunts, in-laws, boyfriends, grandparents and parents and kids and dogs have to step through this waterfall to get inside, like a kind of baptism.

We shut the door. It's dark under there, and it smells of damp earth and wet panting dogs, like we've been returned to some primeval cave dwelling, our electronic senses snuffed out. Not so far from the Sea Islanders after all.

I'm listening for the tornado, but what does a tornado sound like? A blood-curdling scream? The chugging roar of an oncoming freight train? Will we hear trees snapping, hear the skeleton of the house creak and stretch and finally break away? Nobody has told us what to expect, acoustically speaking.

Then, in the darkness, the glow of a small screen. My mother has pulled out her smartphone, and she's pulling up the weather channel's radar. We all gather round, taking comfort in the light, this last vestige of our control over what happens to us.

Don't Worry, I Saw the Doppler

After my visit with Mock, I began collecting tidbits of hurricane folklore online. From a National Oceanic and Atmospheric Administration report written in the days of the typewriter, I learned of a ghostly "Gray Stranger" who wandered the coast warning of impending storms. Supposedly, as a hurricane approaches, alligators bellow ominously and roosters crow in the middle of the night.

The longer I surfed the web in search of Carolinian lore, the harder it was to ignore the irony of getting to know my bioregion this way. In the ecosystem of the internet, electrons flash through networks like hummingbirds, vibrant and swift, bearing tidings of hurricanes present and past from server farms near and far. (The next time a storm follows Hugo's path through South Carolina, it will pass directly over Google's major data center in Moncks Corner.) They have the frantic metabolism of hummingbirds too, drawing energy from fossil fuels. Which means that even as I seek to learn the vernacular of this place I change it, altering the weather conditions I'm trying to describe.

We now know that the conditions of place are unstable: sea levels and temperatures, rainfall patterns, growing seasons. The vernacular can't be recorded in an almanac or passed down from farmer to child. It exists as a dataset to be graphed over time and extrapolated into an uncertain future. The technological changes that allow us to see our homes on a map as the tornado approaches, that allow us to trace a future shoreline given parameters of carbon emission and temperature change, are leading to the creation of a new vernacular of disaster, a language that stretches from the local to the global. It's a kind of creativity arising from destruction, or at least the threat of destruction. We are being forced to respond to the changing nature of what it means to live locally, for better and for worse.

I'm now a member of a new bioregional community of sorts: the listserv for weather-related warnings from the state climate office. Mark Malsick, the Severe Weather Liaison, sends email updates on the status of approaching storms, complete with images and a compelling prose style that mixes the humorous and technical:

Good Morning. Quick update on our friend in the Gulf of Mexico. All hat, no cattle. The closed low that formed over Cuba earlier this week continues to drift glacially northwest with nary a whiff of intensification. This morning's infrared imagery shows just a large, unimpressive blob o'convection near the center with no other features suggesting internal organization. A strong ridge of high pressure to the NNE, coolish GoMex waters, and mid-level dry air entrainment will continue to inhibit any intensification. None, zip, nada. This feature will continue to sashay NNW over Louisiana this weekend and slowly dissipate next week. ... Easterly winds courtesy of this feature will continue this weekend, dragging in moist air off the ocean (pond, with ego…) which should contribute to weekend scattered afternoon rain showers and isolated thunderstorms, nothing severe.

What is a *closed low*? Or *internal organization*? Or *mid-level dry air entrainment*? I wondered. How long will it take before I don't blink with incomprehension at insider lingo like *GoMex*? How long before my fellow Midlanders are chatting about convection blobs as they wait in the grocery store line? Malsick's updates begin with the global, segues to the regional, and then wind up at the local, making me aware of a weather system that extends beyond my senses, beyond the particulars of my immediate surroundings — the clouds I can see, the dry air that curls my hair, the wind that makes the crocodiles bellow.

Living in the Midlands has often produced a jolt of bioregional detail: suddenly I become aware of vines stitching the canopy of pines and oaks, and dark middens beneath the magnolia trees, their fallen leaves like unglazed pottery. Not long ago, a black snake longer than my femur slashed across the road, coiled into a dogwood and disappeared into the trunk as if it never existed. I had to circle the tree twice to find the hole, narrowing my attention to the burlap texture of the bark.

Even as the local ecology comes into focus, however, the listserv has made me feel as if the boundaries of my home have expanded beyond state or national borders. The accessibility of meteorological data changes my sense of the bioregional riskscape. I need to care about what Cuba and the Antilles are experiencing, about what's brewing in that oceanic expanse where storms are born, a space that previously meant nothing to me, that simply didn't exist on any mental map I'd ever made. Whereas our forebearers had no warning of an impending hurricane, and thus no local language of prediction, now we have access to a whole new spectrum of information, visual and linguistic, giving voice to a strange new experience of place.

I've already felt myself itching for the chance to point at the sky and say, "Don't worry, I just saw the Doppler. There's no closed cells in our area." Many people, I suspect, will know what I mean in the not too distant future.

We'll have a vernacular of disaster, a local and global language for orienting ourselves in the bioregional riskscape. The state has just announced that it will send hurricane updates via Twitter, allowing us to tweet back and forth as storms bear down on us. And yet, there will be many who won't speak the language, who, like the thousands who drowned on Sea Island in 1893, will have no warning.

The Storm's Passing

In my sister's yard, there are no broken limbs or sheared off trees. The tempest has left more sinister signs in its wake: yellow tufts of fiberglass insulation like soggy mushrooms in the grass, black twizzles of roofing tile, small shards of wooden rafters, studded with nails. These are fragments of a story ripped from its context — at least, a story we can't read from here, with our senses alone.

On the television, scenes of disaster. A home improvement store roof yanked into the parking lot. Brick apartment complexes reduced to rubble, cars crunched by power lines and trees. The first responders are just arriving, but it's clear from the live helicopter footage that some dwellings are so damaged, anyone inside didn't survive. I feel relieved for my family, but also outraged, as if the tornado has violated the terms of living in place. We were spared, but why? It makes no bioregional sense: weren't those neighborhoods carved from the same blanket of skinny loblolly pines as ours? Why that freeway exit, those stoplights, that minimall?

The storm remains nameless. If there's a language to describe what's happened, it isn't prophetic, and isn't new. Wandering around the yard, picking up debris and trying to imagine how far its come and what its source looks like now, I think of the Sea Islanders, clinging to life in a churning maelstrom of water and wind, praying for dawn. My mother checks in at work. My sisters are calling friends. My brother-in-law, too. I think of all the cell phones that must be ringing now in all the neighborhoods around us, down all the streets and cul de sacs, in all the parking lots, the phones jingling and vibrating, an electrical storm of its own kind. This storm too will gradually abate, until there's just the sound of the phones that nobody answers, ringing in the incomprehensible darkness.

Under The Rainbow of The Chicken Man
By Thomas Maluck

There was not enough color
to be sold in a can,
not after passing the stand
of the funky Chicken Man.

Where once I rode in the smell
of misty Saluda and pines,
that river's strength stands tall
in a watercolor Martin Luther King
the size of a wall.

Somehow, the lesser celebrity
heard in Cola bars and bistros
on the accordion, guitar, and sock-hop
have been found in the glittering hand,
wavy hair, and infectious beat
of a finger-painted King of Pop.

Secondary hues adorn the Chicken-American flag,
but they run no less true than the red white and blue,
old Blood-Stained Banner hung on a pole,
a cross of stars bent to the side –
in their droop, the Chicken Man's smile grows wide.

When he feels traditional,
there is no submission he'll
regret to decorate, with a palmetto tree
first-rate and cool,
red and gold and silver too,
casting shadows on the wall,
and now I want to own them all.

Before the Divorce

- Iris Festival, Sumter, South Carolina
By Julie E. Bloemeke

We came for the flowers
You needed to breathe
them, you said, to fill
with the decadence of color.

I passed the jewelry booth.
You stopped for the stone.
It winked in your palm,
half amethyst, half citrine.

How I wanted you
to have it, to see it shining
around your neck:

a medal for my loneliness,
an admission of your unwept heart.

Instead, you touched it goodbye.

We moved on, searching
for that field of violet and gold,
the banner reason for celebration.
We leaned over walkways, caught

in the hallucination of green.
Sometimes we claimed
purple pulse—see, there?—
in the distance. But as we moved closer
it was, again, a trick of light.

US-321—circle you are subtle
By Zach Mueller

in that you have always existed
as the same equation of a few

odd-something miles along roads
that have always gotten you around—

numbers extending over to subsequent
numbers, white signs visible only through

passing window panes of hand-me-down
Lumina sedans, with the ac blowing along

each mile of brown and tan faded shades
of unnamed weeds on the side of the highway.

It blows slightly as you pass, bending—
like you bend—towards whoever goes by.

You count only what you recognize—
pine, ivy, pavement—like candles

on a birthday cake. But you stop counting.
Not every name is worth knowing.

You can't be new to this world forever
but those pine trees will always be pine,

so long as you're around
to notice.

Tiny Predators

By Darien Cavanaugh

Walking through the statehouse grounds at night, we found
The monument to slavery, the familiar
Black sketch of the famous black ship filled with
All those black bodies crammed together in an orgy
Of misery. We tried to count them but could not
Agree on a number. There were just so many of them.

We moved on, past the wall of black history,
Until we came to the capitol steps.
You pointed up and said, "Look. Night hawks."
I'd always thought those were the old drunks
At the end of the bar at the end of the night,
But you explained that they were real, live
Hawks the size of hummingbirds, tiny predators
You could hold and crush in your hand.

You touched my arm for the last time as we stood
There watching them weave the night sky
In long, slow arcs before cutting and diving
To snatch a smaller life to feed off of, a life itself
Fed by something even smaller, something lost
Among the flood lights that shone up from the copper dome
And pushed through the clouds before giving in
To the moon and a million stars. It was a hard beauty
To see, remembering what we left only a few steps behind.

The Delta

By Matthew Boedy

I remember everything from that last day I spent with Tommy, my older brother, who would go somewhere and die in a war. I spent most of the day—that Sunday when everybody else was with God—trying to show Momma she was wrong about me.

Tommy had stolen five dollars from Momma's purse and wanted to get some food across the highway from where we lived at the Delta Motel. I pleaded with him to wait for me and then ran into our room and shut the door.

I fell to my knees at the sink counter and opened the cabinet below. On the backside of the door I had taped a picture I had quietly ripped from a magazine at Wal-Mart the day before. Tommy had gone off to the bathroom and I needed something to do. A few pages into one that had sex tips on the cover I saw myself in ad—brown hair, same shade of green in the eyes, and my nose, the stubby nub of a nose I claimed came from the father I never met.

All that summer I had asked Momma to let me get my ears pierced and she refused. And being 14 I could not do it without her. Being 14, a month away from high school, I thought I was ready to make my appearance as a woman. I had asked Momma to show me or at least let me use some of the stuff she kept in that Winn Dixie bag underneath the sink. I had asked her each time she caught me going through the bag. She told me her baby girl—"the one I'm supposed to keep from all I did"—didn't need any of that. When I got my period the year before, I showed her my bloody panties. Momma told me she would take me to the store, but eventually it was Tommy.

The ad was not how I looked but how I could look. I stood there with a feeling of "could"—a feeling of something different, something of hope. I ran my fingers over the model's face, as if it were there, in texture. I looked around for one of the blue vests and when I did not see anyone, I tore the ad from the magazine. Then I pocketed a pair of clip-on earrings from the jewelry section. After that I tried to slide eyeliner into my pocket. But a blue vest watched too closely.

On my knees listening to Tommy's threats to leave that Sunday, I eyed that ad again. I ran Momma's hairbrush through my hair like I saw her doing. Then I took a tube of lipstick—red velvet—from her plastic bag and ran it over my lips. The first pass felt like one of her good night kisses. Drunk and not sure how far she was from my face, she sometimes missed. All I felt was a mist. At the sink, I couldn't feel the gloss on my lips so I pressed harder and slowly pulled the color along the curve of my lips.

Next I tore the earrings from their small white holder as if I were opening a Christmas present too early. I tossed the trash deep into the cabinet. I took the earrings because they matched the ad—a metallic blue ball connected to a silver clasp. They were the first thing I ever owned, the first thing I stole.

I jumped to my feet and looked at myself in the mirror. After admitting I did the best I could with the time I had, I smiled to the mirror and went outside. Tommy looked at me funny—covering up his widening mouth with his hand and then shaking his head.

"You look like a boy with lipstick and earrings," he said.

His voice then was full of disorder—not like the voice I would later hear in my head. The drawling accent would remain, though with a stature I never got to see in person.

For now, like mine, his voice bore the burdens we shared—drifting in and out, weakened by each pass through them.

I was wearing one of his old shirts—now mine—that had blue and green in the plaid. It lay flat on me because I had yet to find my figure, though it was beginning to find me. I was wearing shorts that came from his jeans and a pair of Momma's flops. The clothes were all I had clean.

"Why you put on all that stuff anyway? We just going to Wendy's," Tommy said.

"I'm old enough." I remember my voice then being young, like it was still finding its way. I don't remember if I liked it but I suppose then I didn't like very much at all about me. I had wit, though.

"We just going down the street," my brother said.

"Momma say you could use all that of hers?"

"She say you could have that five?"

He started walking then, me behind him. The Delta was off Old Orangeburg Road. It was a four-lane road, with an interstate exit (complete with fenced overpass). Since we had lived at the motel, which had to be since I was 10, we watched the Chinese food come, the drive-up bank come, the do-it-yourself car wash come, and we saw the houses come. When the houses came the road was widened to look like an actual highway.

The Delta's sign—a green palm tree next to red letters—stood between two small brick pillars. It had a row of 32 brick rooms with white doors, each with either a gold plated number on it or the shadow of the digit, opposite the office. While a few rooms were occasionally occupied, we three shared one room. Tommy had one double and I slept with Momma in the other.

The Delta had long ago given up its calling as a tourist stopover. It was no longer listed in AAA. The only remnant of the days when it first opened (before the coming of the interstate system) was what looked like a postcard, blown up to the size of a large map, tacked to a board behind the office counter. The picture was all green and pine and blue and sky with patches of yellow and pink on the ground. Bleached rock lined the driveway where cars—Road Runners and Ramblers, Tommy told me once—were parked. When I looked at the framed print I pictured myself standing underneath the tall sign. I was waving to the cars passing by, always holding someone's hand, and never knowing whose.

The motel was too far from the city to have much trouble. It rented weekly and monthly so we often got the homeless husband or abused wife. And it was just like we learned in school. The delta is the place where the great rivers of the world end. The end of the journey for the sticks and mud and waste. The dumping ground. There was fertile ground there, too. But I never saw it the way Tommy did.

He saw the interstate—like the gulf where the river flowed—as the Delta's opening to the world. That summer Tommy and I often would walk up along the road on the sandy shoulder. We would stop on the overpass and watch the cars rush to anywhere. He said they were always going somewhere and he wanted somewhere to go, too.

We lived in the middle of somewhere, South Carolina, next to a road that could take you everywhere. But we never went. I never went, I say now.

That summer when Tommy told us he was quitting school to join the army, Momma and I asked why. He said he had to go, to be where there was something for him to do. There was something for him out there. I knew that then. I knew what was here at the Delta, here at the dumping ground, the intersection of freedom and desperation.

He explained to us that if anything good was going to happen to him, he had to leave. His leaving was more than about him, though. His father left for the first desert war after giving his part of Tommy to our mother. Momma told Tommy (who later told me when I asked if we had the same father) that his father died in that war. Tommy did not know anything about his father except for that. After he had told Momma, he told me as we stood on the overpass that he was going because his father went.

Tommy was a lean, tall boy, in ROTC, and had no particular physical attribute to remember him by. If I had seen a picture I might say he had his father's nose. He had perfect vision, a perfect heart rate, and could do as many push-ups as you wanted in a minute. He never had a girlfriend, never drank, and never smoked.

And he always beat me across the highway.

"Randy still taking you to the army?" I asked as Tommy waited for me to catch my breath from crossing the highway on a sprint.

When we left that day Momma was still sleeping with Randy, the owner of the Delta. In their room. It was more like his room—Momma just slept there once a week. Once a week for four years. I asked Tommy once why they didn't just take the room next door to us. He said they didn't want us to hear them. I thought they were telling secrets, talking about birthday presents, or something like that.

I followed Tommy into the door next to the drive-thru and stood in line. It was near 11 then. There were a few customers inside, two at the register.

"She didn't have any more than that five in there?" I asked as we stood waiting our turn. He shook his head.

Randy was taking Tommy to the bus station because Momma didn't have a car or a job that summer. I always thought (until Tommy told me) that when Momma was out of work she lived off his father's benefits but they were never married.

She had worked at a hospital before we moved to the Delta and we lived in an apartment closer to the city. When we lived there, we would eat breakfast at the hospital on Saturdays. She would wash my hair in one of those large hospital sinks. And she said if we ever moved again I would have my own room. How we came to the Delta I do not remember, but I remember Tommy telling me we came to the Delta because Momma wanted to marry Randy.

When we got to the front of the line, I leaned over the counter a little to see if any boys were working the grill. But it was all girls with an older man who seemed to hover over their shoulders.

"I'll get us something," Tommy said as he pulled me from the counter. "Go get some ketchup."

I filled three of those small paper cups with ketchup and walked to the table Tommy was. He had some fries and a large order of nuggets we were to share. We shared a drink, too. We liked Dr. Pepper.

"How long before you get sent over there?" I asked after I sat down.

"Not long. Probably weeks, a month or two. I'll send you a postcard. One with a picture of those palaces we took over."

I started noticing that after Tommy decided to enlist that he started using more pronouns. We took over. We are going to be over there a while. We go where they tell us.

I was dipping fries into the ketchup and wiping my mouth all the while unaware I was losing my look.

"You know that comes off when you use a nap…." Tommy said.

I picked up my crumbled napkin and looked at the smears of red velvet and tomato red.

I slowly pulled the earrings from my lobes and set them in the napkin.

"They look like they hurt," Tommy said.

I curled one of my lobes in my finger as a massage. I looked at Tommy and he looked at the road.

"You gonna write me?" he asked after a short silence.

I nodded.

"I'll send you a letter when I get an address—probably after basic, when we get our orders to go. Then we'll know where we will be."

I remember that as a promise and also a lie. The first letter Tommy was to mail sat without postage in his personal effects—what the chaplain and the colonel who came to tell us brought with them.

Coming across the road back to the Delta we noticed a van in the lot—not next to a room but parked near the front office. Momma was coming across from the office to our room and we followed her inside.

"Where you two been?" she asked.

"We went to Wendy's," I said.

"With whose money?"

Then I looked at Tommy and he looked at Momma.

"I guess it don't matter now. The bastard's selling out," Momma said.

Tommy picked up on it before I did.

"You mean to those people in that car?" he said as he pushed back the curtains to eye the Indian man and his wife getting into their mini-van.

"He didn't tell me 'til the last day," she said. "They're buying all the motels, living in them, and bringing over their families."

I remember after we came inside our room, I sat down on the bed and Momma sat next to me and put her arm around me. Her hair was not like mine—I could see it dry as hotel toilet paper and hanging from her head like ten strands of paper towel tore from the same roll. Her eyes were wet and worn.

"Maybe we can find somewhere you can have your own room," she said.

She looked over at Tommy.

"He's still taking you tomorrow while we clear out," she said.

Tommy kicked the leg of the chair and held up two fingers.

"He couldn't give you two weeks? After all this? Not even two weeks? And with all that you and him …"

I suppose I knew it before then. But after Tommy failed to finish that sentence, I knew what Momma had done for sure. I understood, then, too that Tommy lied when he told me about marriage. Momma stood up next to Tommy and tried to ease his anger. I felt a tear form in each eye and I looked in the mirror—smudged lips, wet eyes, and crumpled ears. I felt my face in the mirror—the skin and texture absent from my hand, lost. I saw my hand move down my cheek but did not feel it.

I sniffled and Momma came back to sit next to me. I was in the middle of using my sleeve to finish what the napkin had started. Momma then noticed the remnants of the lipstick. She grabbed my cheeks with both hands and turned my face to hers.

"Let me see what you doing …" Her words seemed ready for anger but her voice felt sorry for me. "What you got on?"

Tommy got out words before me.

"She got all that stuff on and she ruined it with her napkin at Wendy's."

His voice did not feel sorrow for me.

I tried to smile but Momma's hands were still tight on my cheeks. She pushed my face back for a better view and then turned it side to side.

"Of all the days to go putting on make-up. …Of all the times to … want to be ..."

The ad flashed in my mind at that moment. Of all the times to want to be beautiful.

"You get all this from my bag?" she asked.

I shook my head and drew from my pocket the crumpled napkin. I flicked it open and revealed the earrings.

"Where you get these from? Clip-ons … I swear. You've

been wanting piercing, I know, child, but you got to go and take some sorry clip-ons?"

I was a child that summer. Not because of my age but because of what I didn't know. Momma's face—full of astonishment at my ignorance—showed me what I lacked. I did not know so many things.

Momma took the earrings from my napkin and clenched them in her hand. She kept whispering, "Some sorry clip-ons."

The earrings were the first thing I owned. They were the first thing I stole, too, but you can never own something you steal. Like stealing hope from a magazine. It is never really yours, but you think it is.

I learned that on that last day I spent with Tommy, the last day he spent in the Delta.

Neighbors

Columbia, SC

By Nicola Waldron

There are places the sidewalk's dropped away,
where the leavings of dogs, hard, white,
lie unburied in our way.
Someone's left a board beside the road,
left in the board the long nails that held together once
a cupboard or a chair.

If you're not watching, if you're wearing
the wrong kind of shoe, you can turn
your ankle here.

Across from those boards, that dirt, lives a man
with three dogs, each one a different breed,
who polishes his guns, looking up at the snouts
while his dogs force their faces through the wire,

and this, perhaps, is why my little boy
climbs up inside the stroller when we pass,
squeals his resistance.

At the far end of the street
live two more boys his age,
well groomed, sweet faced,
who will not play with him.

Perhaps we seem to them
like those dogs across the way—alien, unclean, hungry—
straining at the fence
to sniff at them.

Manifest Destiny
By Dianne Turgeon Richardson

Memphis and Tupelo in an afternoon haze,
Birmingham by supper, Atlanta in darkness,
watching the sky lighten over Aiken County I-20.
My frontier rolls along through pine barrens and sand fields,
marsh grass and black water streams,
Atlantic stretches and early sunrises,
the familiar call of the eastern landscape.
I have seen America and the question is not what's out there.

I pull into my mother's driveway
at breakfast, and she is waiting.
The air is already thick,
green needles quivering, blades of centipede grass vibrating,
scrub oaks dropping September acorns underfoot,
the movements of a Carolina homecoming.

Sound

You Stay in Columbia or are Forgotten with Adluh Flour

By Brandi L. Perry

If you stay inside after days of cypress knees,
days without slippery bricks or hell yeahs,
cascading days empty of sweat and smooth isolation
or a close bank of cicadas putting off lightness,
will I dissuade you that the highways were coming to me?

Why reach to the window or the cotton mill fizzle,
to galoshes pushing backward under steaming manholes?
How are they of such lightness that they stop a river, besides?
Congaree whispers grayscale, plants take solace outside
a pale wash of fleas and ticks, then the lintheads cough,

all without their spitting rags, every pain and exultation,
every sorrow or joy separating breaths.
What is this South that would sweep
Palmetto bugs through its screened door
or take you to a silent film you were allowed to listen to?

A woman was swell hipped or walked out the door,
a girl was slender of wrist or walked out the door.
Is there another opening – a table and a chair or anything –
perhaps some hummingbird cake? And are you certain?
What cannot transcend such formlessness?

Outside this life, a visible life that forgets,
we discover the nothing you are: the deliverer,
certainly – but also not the deliverer.
We go from the window and listen and listen
and we hear them – the workers. They go toward this death.

We come away from our factories in front of the cannons,
in front of the white columns, behind the blue darkness
which both thins us and enlarges us.
We haven't undone the evil bargain for our play
of several generations. We haven't reduced it.

We've only thickened it like aged molasses.
I drop the rickety footbridge and forget about it.
I remember with them and they stop singing or laughing
or talking altogether. Everything is wrong. They reject me.
I can't run you from Columbia or quiet you, my history.

When We Stopped Talking About the Weather

By Ray McManus

Language itself is just dust, crystalline particles, a blue snow descending in silence. - Campbell McGrath

This country life has a limited vocabulary – call it rural, full of foul language,
tracks dug in with more fences to ride, more horses to break. It's full of itself.
When you were wild, you learned real fast that the secret to any pony is
survival; you believed the rope was a miracle, and learning to let go was just
enough to discover God. But no matter how much you want to climb, the dust
and sage and granite, won't let you go there – no God, no heaven dotted in crystalline
patterns, just heat and sand gone too far. This place won't die easy, only in bits, in particles,
in stories braided in tongue. The forest becomes a field, the field becomes a plot, a
fire, an escape, a chimney left standing, a finger poking a hole in a blue
sky, then rain. There is the myth of dreams – flooded pastures will never fill with snow.
There is the dirt road, its path rutted and forever. There is your frontier descending
into pine and sparkleberry, fractured in the fall. There is the sheet you'll be buried in –
a thicket, a briar song, a mouth of honey and dirt, a drift, a rattle, the damp silence.

Mare

By Ivan Young

She pulls loose strands
of tassled moss, stretches

her muscled neck over
the redwood fence planks.

Her black eyes watch me,
tail twitching at flies, ears honed.

She startles at each move I make,
Muscles taut, eyes tracing the path

to the tack room where bit
and bridle hang. He clips her

to lines stretched from the wall,
tries to assure me--*she's untrainable,*

she threw you. And then he motions
for me to leave. Even as I sidestep

piles of dung, I can hear
my grandfather work the lever,

the ratchet of the casing
pushing into place. I am small

puffs of pasture dust, I am
the echo of the shot bouncing

across the field, I am the noose
of lead-rope I've forgotten I still hold.

Neighbor

By Lauren Allen

Country dogs bark, urgent to indicate a stranger. Someone bangs on the door, not the polite rapping of an unexpected visitor. The neighbor hesitates in porch light shadows, the smell of whiskey shoves inside. *I killed her.* Whippoorwills and frogs rehearse their spring chorus but Orion still stalks the frosted sky. The flashlight skips ahead of footsteps muffled by pine straw crushed to felt by tires. The shrill crescendo rises—stops. Walk toward, shrink away, dread the discovery of a dead woman: Mary gunshot. Mary throat slit. Mary beaten to oblivion.

Riff

for James Brown

By Kevin Simmonds

Heavy on the one
    That way

Sun's halves
    Hi hat

Diesel brass
    Burned black

Pretty pleased
    Every one

Music and Dancing Atop Arsenal Hill

By Kristine Hartvigsen

Anyone strolling Finlay Park on a temperate Saturday evening in downtown Columbia easily could be enchanted by the distant wooing of fiddle, tinwhistle, and bodhran wafting down over the commons from Arsenal Hill Community Center. What is this, you wonder, and redirect your path toward the music. There's a purplish hue to the horizon, as the sun set just a while ago. The open windows of the community center glow invitingly against the advancing dark. The mild temperatures are agreeable to your sleeveless arms. As you near the spare white building at the top of the rise, a lively Irish reel in 4/4 time pulls you further, and you must peek inside. What you see nearly transports you to another century.

The diminutive, one-room building has become every bit an 18th-century dance hall, barring the overhead electric lights, of course. The room is awash in movement, men and women gliding swiftly across the sprung wood floor interacting with each dancer in their path. They smile pleasantly and gaze directly into one another's eyes, stomp their feet in unison and melt into a long swing for 16 counts, eyes locked, seemingly enraptured. Many of the ladies sport long A-line peasant skirts that flow out appealingly as they twirl. The men, hands gentle at their partners' lower backs, guide the women toward the next couple, and they commence into a "ladies chain" in which the women reach across the aisle and join hands, pulling and passing by one another to be greeted and turned by the opposing gentlemen. It is so splendid and elegant that you cannot stop watching. But join in? It looks too difficult. How do the dancers know where to go in the chaotic stream of people? How do they avoid collisions? You needed only to arrive a few minutes earlier to witness the dance from the very beginning. Then you would have seen a person known as a "caller" walk the dancers through several steps and practice the choreographed figures several times, to be repeated over and over throughout a 10-to-15-minute piece of music, before the first note emanated from the stage.

The friendly folks resting and using hand towels to wipe sweat from their necks and foreheads did not arrive by horse or buggy but more likely by Prius or Beetle. And they're more likely to be accountants, therapists, IT managers, or even chefs than they are to be blacksmiths, cobblers, or stationers. And the more you observe, you realize you have not actually stepped back in time. The Ramones t-shirt, the tie-dye skirt, and the Birkenstock sandals spotted here and there among the dancers soon set that notion to rest. But there's a feeling here that is timeless. An inescapable camaraderie seems to bring these people together, if only for a few hours a month. Their bond is a combined love of music, movement, and their fellow man.

The Columbia Traditional Music and Dance Society hosts these seasonal, monthly "contra dances" at Arsenal Hill. Novices always are welcome, and basic moves or figures, such as allemande, do-si-do, gypsy, promenade, and balance and swing are taught and practiced before the dance begins. The individual moves may seem familiar, and you soon suspect (to your horror) that they must be square dancing. Traumatized memories from 6th grade gym class come to mind. Though a square dance may be thrown in on occasion, these parallel line formations are quite different. You're not likely to see the stereotypical ruffled petticoats or scarf ties here. It's basically come as you are, but wear comfortable, non-scuffing shoes.

Contra dancing actually preceded square dancing in North America by about a century, give or take. The tradition is said to have been brought overseas by those who established the first colonies in the New England region. The dance's origins trace to 17th century English "country dance," the rural common man's adaptation of formal dances exclusive to the privileged few who were welcomed into the royal court during the reign of Elizabeth I. As the popularity of "country dance" spread throughout Europe, the French began calling it "contredanse," and eventually it became known as "contra dance."

In the American colonies, long before the emergence of such modern-day tools as online dating, the main focus of contra dances was social; the dances were mixers. The very nature of contra dancing dictates that couples dance in long lines down the dance hall, progressing in opposite directions, interacting with just about everyone on the floor. To this day, it is considered rude not to make eye contact. Of course, focusing on your partner's eyes also helps assuage any dizziness that may come with continued twirling and spinning.

There are contra dance groups all over the country. Northern states may be best known for their active contra dance scenes. But just up the road, Asheville, North Carolina, is also a well-known hub for contra dancing, which is a big part of the twice-annual Lake Eden Arts Festival in nearby Black Mountain. Greenville also has the Harvest Moon Folk Society, which hosts dances in northern Greenville County, and Charleston also has an active contra scene, including the annual Palmetto Bug Stomp. In the Midlands, Lake Murray also has a dance group. It is only fitting that famously hot Columbia be a contra-friendly city among the many that indulge the dance gypsy in all of us.

Shandon

By Nan Ancrom

it's the casual willow   the robin's flight
no more rough seas the ancestor's scaled
just sluggish drains   stuffed gutters
getting the garbage out on time

among the solid folk the porous poet peers
to gather up what can be learned
at the dawn of afternoon rain   a stiff safety
among the tended lawns   a harbor

the East Village is far behind me
there's no anarchist in sight   it's here
that finally the mind turns toward its right:
restitution   a quiet flowing light

Kayak: A Lake Murray Journal

By Randy Spencer

I

step down cautiously into the shell
single foot first, center of gravity low.
do not disturb the water
lapping underneath

the morning lake is quicksilver
broad, slow swells
sweep from bank to bank
across the cover

push out slowly
quietly, as not to shatter
the water, its glass moment
then feather the paddle to gain air

there is absolute stillness
nothing moves but sound
as birds, unseen, dart noisily tree to tree,
their notes as sharply focuses as the leaves

slip silently into the fog.
the horizon loses traction, crimps beneath the keel.
paddling closer, a single row of pines
rappels against the granite sky

from beneath the water the gaze of a fish,
eyes fixed, the obligation of a stone
listen obliquely
to the ospreys' cries of alarm

II

water cannot distinguish
the paddles dimpled symmetries
from the water strider's
purposeful scurrying

at the cove's outer reach
a small wave crests over a thin shoal of gravel
becomes for a moment
a small tsunami lifting the bow

a green anole
stretches out on a dry buttonbush,
its throaty red luminescence
captures sunlight

under a clabbered sky
a Brownian flight
of mayflies
anchors a river birch

flower-heads of mimosa
float down
pirouette in swirling air
a shimmering stage

shorten the stroke
glide slowly
inside the willow's green trellis
a water snake curls on the rough bark

in the clear water,
hollowed out, closely guarded
a bream bed
stirs up a trove of chalky, broken clamshells

a thin rain
pricks the skin of the cove
circles widen,
disappear

III

at dusk, migratory martins
bob and weave
skim over the water,
first three, then a dozen, then uncountable numbers

through a narrow opening
an early moon
visible through the slender trees,
an archetypal resistance to darkness.

flints of stars
strike across the night's cold steel,
sparks dance
helter-skelter in the black water

hauled up, overturned,
the empty kayak
squats like a disgruntled terrapin
trailing sinewy lake water

a single mockingbird
fills
the night air
with stolen song

What the Moon Say

From the roof of the then abandoned Olympia Mill

By Robbie Pruitt

I watched the moon from the roof of an old mill in the city.

Nightfall is near, time to disappear—
like the times and the people of this vacant scene.

The moon says, "I watched you when you were born,
I watched you live, and I will watch you when you die."

The moon knows its course and it's going to run it.

Neighbor

*But he, willing to justify himself, said unto Jesus,
And who is my neighbour?*

By Ed Madden

Our neighbor David's a man on a mission,
going on and on at the neighborhood meeting
about the Lord and how the crippled men
in the MS house next door need him.

He was dismissed, he says, from his job
for commenting on a woman who was dressed,
he says, *like a whore*. He took it to court
and won, he says, when the woman showed up

there in something that looked like underwear.
Proved his point. He used to go over to read
the Bible to the men next door, till some guy's sister
complained when he told a smoker he already had

one disability, so why would he want another?
We eat our chili, look at each other.

A Brief History of Bowling

By Laurel Blossom

Objects found in the grave of an Egyptian boy may belong
    to a crude form of bowling.
The objects, found in 1930, date from 3200 B.C.

In the Dark Ages, bowling determined if you had sinned.
Martin Luther preached, however, that even if you rolled
    a gutter ball, all was not lost.

King Edward III banned bowling, a distraction from 100
    years of archery practice.
Henry VIII played nine-pins.

In downtown New York it's still called Bowling Green.
Consider the legend of Rip van Winkle.

Connecticut outlawed nine-pins because it attracted gambling.
Somebody invented ten-pins.

Remember "Bowling for Dollars?"
The White House installed its first bowling alley in
    what is now the Situation Room.

1968, Orangeburg, South Carolina:
Police killed three black students protesting segregation
    at a local bowling alley.

Ancient Polynesians rolled stones the length of a bowling lane (60 feet).
Herman Melville set pins in Hawaii.

Excerpt from *South: A Memoir*
By Nicola Waldron

I return from watching, in England, my maternal grandmother die. I have to skip the funeral to get back to South Carolina in time to begin my job at a federally funded program housed on the edge of the university in Columbia, the state capital. Each afternoon for five weeks, I am to report for duty as the creative writing instructor for two classes of teens. My students are first generation college hopefuls, high school kids who want to better themselves and need a hand up. I understand that here in the South that means they will mostly be black, though I assume there'll be some poor white kids too, one or two Hispanics, perhaps: a representative smattering.

"I've always wanted to do this kind of work," I've persuaded the interviewer, because I have. "I was a scholarship kid myself," I say. On the form, I've actually quoted Gandhi: "Be the change you want to see in the world." The pallor of my skin, I'm aware, might be an issue, but surely the color wheel will spin us all into a centrifugal blur once it gets going, once we get to know each another. This is what I have learned from my years in London, from that city's highly spiced, multicultural soup.

I leave my own small children trapped inside the house with the sitter I've found at the last moment, a friendly girl—does it matter that she's black?—who has a cool new cell phone that dazzles them, and I pray that our outdated air-conditioning will hold out. I pull on a sun protective shirt—surely the ugliest clothing known to mankind—and climb on my bike, determined to shape up and save money, to mitigate in pathetic measure the effects of all the driving we do, ferrying the children back and forth to the school of choice at which we've enrolled them, the school that lies on the other side of town and is 80% white, unless you count the teachers, in which case it's more like a 95-5 split. On the morning of Obama's election, I've looked in vain for someone with whom to share a victory smile.

My new job pays miserably—a fact I've checked only after I've accepted it, just like South Carolina is a place I've come to only after the fact, my husband having accepted a position at the university with me in an extreme state of pregnancy. But I am resolved: surely the money I'll earn is more than most of my students' parents make, and slightly more than I'll pay the sitter, who I've already bargained down to $12 an hour (the going rate is $10), afterwards feeling guilty when I see the condition of her car.

Who am I?

As I bump over the railway tracks towards the poorer end of the university campus, the thick layer of sunscreen I've plastered onto my ill-adapted Celtic skin begins to melt and run into my eyes. Without it, I will cook: I will contract skin cancer and die. A line of sweat forms around the band of my helmet, collects at the back of my neck and trickles down my spine, coming to rest in a pool between my buttocks. "Disgusting," I say out loud. "That feels *disgusting*." In England, I was often exceedingly wet, rain-drenched, or even on occasion too hot, but no one ever suffered the two states at the same time.

Though the program I'm to teach on is run by the university, it is housed in a warehouse-like edifice opposite the old gym that's patronized only by junior faculty and poorly paid staff—those who can't afford the shining new Strom Thurmond Wellness Center down the road, a grand mausoleum of stone and glass finished the year before we arrived.

My husband told me about it as a sweetener, a way to soften the blow of moving here, but that was before we saw the fee schedule.

I'm told the Booker T. Washington Building recently survived a fire, but no one will talk about who might have started it. No one tells me, either, that this was a beloved, historic black high school, closed thirty-six years earlier to a furor: that most of the school was demolished without any plan to rebuild it or properly commemorate its importance. Now, as a result of the conflagration, boxes of salvaged books and equipment line the hallways. I'm reminded of the fourth-floor room I rented in South London in my mid-twenties: no heat, no proper stove, no door to the bathroom; no fire escape.

I make a mental note to read up on Mr. Washington, for I have no clear idea who he is or what role he played in American history; what place he holds in the consciousness of black southerners, or white ones for that matter. I've only just got my Sherman and Lee straight. I'm only interested, I think as I climb the long flight of steps to the main floor, now that I have something at stake.

Inside the program office, a sparsely equipped center of operations, a group of impeccably dressed black women greets me with polite if distant kindness. They glance sidelong at my bike gear and red face and direct me to the girls' bathroom, where I change and make a speedy exit just as the students arrive in an adolescent clatter. I stash my things in the corner, like Thomas Hardy's Tess Durbeyfield hiding her farm boots under a bush so that she can arrive inconspicuous at the town dance, the difference being that no one here, not even the most desperate soul, will steal my sweat-soaked clothes and ancient running shoes. Most of them, I'm pretty sure, won't have heard, either, of Tess or her creator: just as Booker T. Washington and an embarrassing number of other well-known African-American figures remain unknown to me.

I wobble down the hallway in the bargain heels I bought back in Chicago, our last place of residence. Filene's Basement, brownish-black with a pointed toe; surprisingly comfortable. I've been allocated a big white classroom lined with thirties' style windows that do nothing to keep the heat at bay. The room's inhabited by a motley assortment of lecture-style chairs, the kind with a little table attached that traps you in, God help you if you're big. None of my students has arrived yet, so I push the chairs into a large circle, as perfectly formed and unbroken as I can make it. I'm expecting twenty-four young men and women in each group, twice what I'm used to. It's absolutely silent in the building, except when the ancient air conditioners snarl and rattle into action. I wait.

I spread out my papers and unstrap my watch. I swagger back and forth, peering out through the little window in the door. Eventually, I push my way out and go looking. I glance at my purse as I leave, wondering if it will be safe there on its lonely chair—the only thing in the room of any useful value. By moving southwards, the habits of a lifetime have, all at once, become suspect.

I risk it.

I stride down the hallway in the direction of the offices, and hear voices slipping out from under the doors of the big auditorium. Doubling back, I peek in to see a vast crowd of teenagers, talking animatedly. When they see my face, they look up, stop momentarily, then go back to their conversations and cell-phones. I step inside and try to make myself imposing, a role I've never played well. "Creative writing?" I bellow, adopting my fearless Jean Brodie persona. A few reluctant nods. "Follow me!" and the crowd, grudgingly, emerges, until I'm treading water in a sea of moody-looking boys and chatty girls, who buzz with the thrill of having missed so much class time. I've forgotten how big a fifteen-year-old boy can be, though when I meet the eyes of the young man closest to me, I can see the child gazing out, clear and sad and hopeful. I smile and he doesn't smile back, something I've already learned to expect when a black face meets my unwelcome white one, or indeed when a local of either race hears I'm not from these parts. I'm not even a damn Yankee like my husband, and it seems no one quite knows how to categorize me.

A skinny girl in flat-ironed ringlets and a brightly colored, Bolivian style waistcoat barrels up to me, pulling her friend along by the sleeve. I used to wear clothes like that, I think, things just a little bit out-of-the-ordinary, exotic; not enough to draw too much attention. On her, the look is decidedly cute.

"Hello!" I say, a touch too loud.

She narrows her eyes in response. "Are *you* our teacher?"

"Yes, I'm Nicola. What's your name?" We are exactly the same height, small.

She shoots her friend a cool glance, then pulls back her chin. "You *foreign*?" she asks extravagantly, pulling back her pretty shoulders, raising her wary brow.

I remind myself I'm almost three times her age and have no reason to feel unnerved, but the obvious differences in our origins circle above us like the hawks that frequent the squirrel-infested pines of our local park–we've seen one, with the children, snatch one of the unsuspecting critters clean out of the branches and whack it against the ground until its head came off.

Like all the other bodies that surround me, the girl's skin is a smooth brown, her hair black, whereas I am freckled puce, topped with the orange-tinged, humidity-frizzed hair that caused my classmates in elementary school to taunt me with 'Ginger.' It was a benign enough epithet, if it hadn't been applied with such biting, impious force.

For what should we settle? Empathy? An attempt at compassion? Silence? But I am here to help these youngsters find their voices, and to share mine: the only way, I believe, to come close.

Around me, the students' collective conversation creates a low, melodious hum quite different from the high, screechy cacophony I remember from my own schooldays. I stand inside it as in a warm ocean, feeling it bubble up, oddly soothing. No one here, I've come to appreciate in the months since we moved, is going to simper or tell me, "I love your accent. I could listen to you all day," something I've learned almost to expect in other parts of the union.

"Come on, then," I say. "Let's go *write!*" and I move off in the direction of the classroom. No one will walk beside me. Instead, they follow in a clump and at a distance not so much respectful as cautious. As if I'm some kind of monitor lizard or cottonmouth snake who might turn and strike at the least justification; at none.

I clip-clop down the hallway, a pied piper without a score, the town's children hesitant at my heels. It would be easy, I consider, for the bodies behind me to stampede.

Close to Nature

By Ruth Varner

From her kitchen window, Jessie Mae noticed a strange pale object hanging from the distant fence surrounding the three acre property. Random trash, she remembered, would catch in the small squares of wire designed to keep a horse's hoof safe from harm. But they'd had no wind, and the thing hadn't been there yesterday.

As daylight broke, curls of fog slipped between the oaks and hickories. The ghostly object absorbed her attention more than the red-headed woodpecker and finches circling their feeder. Curiosity mingled with worry as Jessie Mae set aside her dishtowel. In motions of habit she gathered three dog biscuits to carry to the pups in their pen. Most days the dogs made her smile as they attacked their treats. But her mind was edgy with concern, and she tried to focus on the day's errands with her husband Billy. What was at the fence? At breakfast, she described the object to Billy, whose frown reflected her anxiety. An hour later their SUV eased down the drive. Abruptly they swerved left and drove across the grass to examine the fence.

Jessie Mae gasped as they drew closer. The white object was the belly of a young deer, her rear hoof caught in the fence as she attempted to jump it. No telling how long she'd struggled there. The hoof was nearly severed from the leg but she was alive. Moving to both sides of the fence, the two seniors lifted her, untangled the leg and lowered her gently to the ground. Her wide eyes begged for help but she made no sound. Except for the break at the hoof, there was little blood or obvious trauma to her body. Trembling, she bounded up to run, then crashed to the ground with no support from her hind leg.

Staring at the fence, Jessie Mae eased strained muscles in her back and shook her head. "Just can't believe a fence safe for horses could injure a deer."

"Now what do we do?" asked Billy, wiping blood from his hands to his jeans, "We can't just leave her here. She'll die without help."

His wife punched a number into her cell phone and asked the animal hospital for advice.

"We can't help you," said the receptionist, "Here's the number for the wildlife office."

A quick dial of the number resulted in a long recorded message.

"Is there no help?" Jessie Mae muttered.

Cussing his bad knees, Billy knelt beside the deer and stroked her quivering body. The grey fur felt soft as a child's blanket. Still she made no sound. He struggled to lift her across the street to a wooded lot, her legs kicking sporadically, and settled her in tall grass away from the road. Wide dark eyes followed him.

Billy slammed his fist on the car hood, "Come on, let's ask at the county park. S*omebody* must be able to help."

They glanced at the animal as their car pulled away but there was no movement.

At the park an attendant found the address for the wildlife office, and they rushed to find it. From there an agent working nearby called and agreed to meet them.

A fast ride back to the deer found her unmoved, weary and

broken. Billy paced beside the road while his wife sighed and mouthed a prayer.

In a spray of gravel the wildlife man pulled up and stepped from a mud-splashed truck, one hand on the pistol at his hip.

"Not much hope for these injured animals," he said without emotion. "A group in Spartanburg takes them in and treats them, but this leg looks pretty bad. What do you want me to do?"

The lifetime partners walked toward the trees to talk.

"She looks perfect except for that leg," said Billy, breathing hard. "I don't know what to do. Those eyes haunt me." Stress wrinkled his brow.

For a moment, his spouse was silent. "I don't see how we can help her. Foot injuries are the hardest to heal, and worse keeping a wild animal still." She reached for Billy's work-calloused hand and held it.

"I think we have to do this." Her voice was merely a whisper. His jaw tightened as he stared at his boots, newly stained red across the toe.

The conversation was brief with the man in the truck, who nodded. "Why don't y'all head home now?"

Billy and Jessie Mae crossed the street in silence, one large hand closed around a smaller frail one.

A single gunshot exploded in the still morning air, echoing across the woods and grassy lot.

Moments later the bells of St. Peter's church softly chimed the hour.

Saturday Mornings

By Ray McManus

If I hear children laughing,
I'm mistaken. It's just me
and the neighbor, some rolls
of chicken wire and fence post,
rabbits hanging from the rafters.
I don't remember if I cut myself
on the chicken wire or the fence
post. I don't remember if I cried.

My neighbor takes the last rabbit
out of the cage, holds it by its feet,
and whips it forward. I don't know
if they named the rabbits. I'm eight.
He tells me that it is a myth about rabbits
screaming, but I am not sure I can
believe him, and he yawns as he tosses
a clump onto the table beside him.

Before we moved out here, this was
a prairie for the woods, a tract
for copper tubes and tin so the wild
stayed wild before it was swallowed
by cages and cotton fields. Now
it's 10:00 a.m. and rabbits dangle
and drip on the sandy barn floor
and my neighbor tells me that
rabbits can get as big as dogs,
and up north they eat people.

The Bats

By Ivan Young

Bats appear like weavers
hanging darkness—the sky
and the sky crafted. Their bodies
an absence, muscular curves

in the halo of a street lamp.
They lay out threaded patterns
beneath a quilt of stars like eyes
moving under lids, like eyes

finding some dream stretched
across looms of bracken and reed.
I walk a black Carolina road
of cattails, a stagnant pond.

The hover of mosquitoes
an unbearable treble, sweet
voices full of blood. The bats
a silence stitching at the insects.

One flies so close it stirs
a strand of hair trying to pull
the night out of me, dark angel
that warps and woofs a landscape

below it—moss like old wool,
a house with no lights, the stop sign
that marks that quiet street

where no cars ever turn.

Possum

By Ed Madden

A thumping under the tub, something
rubbing, something getting settled in.

One morning, we could hear a soft snoring.

Later, in the crawl space beneath the house,
we found warped boards in the floor

where the pipes come in—
and a whiff of something, fluff and dead leaves.

One night we woke to growls and hissing, a fight,
maybe mating. *They have forked penises, you know*,

he said. I thought about that as the growls
subsided, and outside, in the dark,

wild things roamed the yards.

Southern Lit after 1900

By Brandi L. Perry

Dr. Powell asks a volunteer to read "Lee in the Mountains"
and I stare at the page, landing on another language,
another place: cypress roots, Blue Ridge, Shenandoah

and antiquated words like *chimney crotch*,
Not knowing that Pickett is General George Pickett
and Davidson is writing about Gettysburg.

There are no toeholds, no footnotes to help fit
tongue to words. Is Appomattox a city, a battle, a river?
I just trained myself to say App-a-lat-chuh not Appa-lay-shuh.

Other students volunteer, move through lead bullet words
that would only misfire in my mouth. They lob terms
like Agrarian, blunt as cannonballs across grassy earth

I scramble to comprehend, to pull meaning from shrapnel.
Text full of new notes – *valley, mountains, river,* Psalms 139,
I still don't understand what it means when I read

Entire student body volunteered for confederate service 1861,
or why there are so many poems about Robert E. Lee.
How brick buildings sag under complicated pasts,

why a federation of white men called themselves Fugitives,
or why the confederate flag still flies at the capitol,
less than a mile from my apartment in the old cotton mill.

Touch

Fishing with Dad

By Jennifer Bartell

The boat slices through water: fractured clouds, blue-skied reflection on a black, glassy surface. Ripples to the shore. Hands grasp for crickets, the prick of their jagged legs, brush of antennas. Crickets too quick. Fingers dig into a can of dirt. The worm twists and contorts, is threaded onto a hook, dangles like an ornament. The best bream be near the shore, near the shade. They nip at my ornament. Winnow it to nothing. But they are slow to bite. We see them gasping for air just on the surface. Hear them splash back down into the deep and muddy waters. This is not like last time, when I charmed thirteen fish onto my hook. When the red worms did not fight. I cast my rod again and again ...

He untwines the line,
casts it back into the unknown waters. No bites.

Pilgrimage

By Lauren Allen

After my sister lulls the babies to bed
we take the dogs out for a walk
down the road we used to gallop
where we knew the fence would help
us pull our horses to a halt.
Past the cow skull that disappeared
long ago but left its name
to mark the spot.
We climb the fence
POSTED NO TRESPASSING.
The trees grow thicker—
guarding, obscuring.
The vines conspire.
We evade the plucks and pricks
of twisted barbed wire.
The dogs run off.
Even our voices desert us
when we find the rusty gate,
the moss-covered granite.
Names lost, births and deaths obliterated,
but the stone hard and enduring.

This marble lamb, kneeling and weathered,
guards the sleep of a child
the same age as the slumbering twins.

Autumn Angels

By Rieppe Moore

Making autumn angels
in the park behind the Municipal Center

not because we were reckless youths
but because

   we were reckless with passion
fainting in the thought that
we would separate

as all the colors would, that
succumb to awkward brunette
bluffs

      harbingers of a winter we
wouldn't have even if we
longed

          for
    the kiss runs dry like the creektide
next to us as a charming vestige.

   Our bodies
lengthened in the angels we made
while the DOT circled our highways.

The Gardener

By Alexis Stratton

To feel the weight of the wet soil in your fingers. The dampness on your palms. To know that your hands are making something that will grow into something good. Something useful.

My father always planted vegetables. We ate out of the garden every summer and took the extra to our neighbors. That was back before South Carolina gave much of a damn about anyone going hungry. Didn't give much of a damn about black people, either. That's what Dad used to say, at least. I grew up at a time when things weren't officially segregated. But it doesn't mean they were much better.

No, maybe that's a lie. Maybe I remember things differently now. Maybe I forget those white neighbors we gave food to. The ones who lived in houses smaller than ours. That didn't have the land in back, a couple acres so the kids could play and their dads plant.

Maybe I never knew what it was like to go hungry. Maybe because of that, I didn't have to hunger after other stuff—my neighbors' stuff. The white kids' stuff on the other side of town. Maybe I learned to be content with enough.

My mother would disagree. She'd tell me about the time when I smacked my sister just to get her to hit me back. She might remind me that I always wanted a brother. She'd say I hated my sister because of it—since she wasn't what I'd wanted.

I could tell her she's wrong, but it wouldn't matter. There's no one to tell now anyway. No house left, Dad remarried. Moved into a city. Not even a window box or some herbs. Nothing to remind him of the soil beneath his fingers.

The faces are gone, and I'm gone, too. And the land beneath me blurs. My mind tells me it's all desert. Nothing good could grow there. But I know what my sister said before I left—"It's the fucking cradle of civilization, Joshua," as if the Garden of Eden were still there now. Or Babylon. I can't remember which she said. One of them. As if it were my fault we were there, as if I didn't know things like she did. Thinks she's something, straight-A student. Protests at the State House. She said she didn't care how often Dad reminded her she's got a brother in the war—"Why don't you take some personal fucking responsibility?"

If mom were still here, she'd wash her mouth out with soap. Always a God-fearing woman, Mom. Well, not God-fearing, but God-loving. She loved and loved, and that's why we knew the neighbors' names and even had white people over for supper. Mom said if you loved enough, the rest didn't matter.

But maybe Ruth is right. I wonder if things could grow here like they do back in Winnsboro. I want to touch the ground and plant a seed and watch it grow. I want to know.

I want to believe that the seed is in the word "freedom." That the *ee*'s will just get bigger and bigger until they take up the whole space beneath me. That we water that word with each takeoff. I imagine seeds dropping from my plane. Imagine that it's not what they tell me it is. That turning over the soil brings new growth.

My sister sent me a care package. It arrived a few days ago. Had some of my favorite candy and a short letter. She said she sent me love. And I felt it in my hands. I remembered. And then I put the letter away. I folded it up. I put it in my pocket. I stepped out onto the deck of the aircraft carrier. I waited.

Taste

Cantaloupe

By Melissa Johnson

Musk like the sheets
upon finding a new lover
in hottest midsummer

fills the whole house
lies oleaginous on the air
orangey, over-ripe.

Bland beige exterior grids
into greenish veins, a tracery
of circulating avenues.

Roughness grabs at fingertips,
pulls them into shallow depressions,
rolls away to omphalos ends, like fontanels.

Slip the knife into little resistance,
hollowness at center—yet the serrations
catch—blade must be drawn through.

Womblike center stuffed with flat
pointed seeds in a web of tissue,
yields to the spoon's curette,

the heavy wetness
onanistically spills
into the sink or bin.

Orange-pink bowls
molded by thin putty-colored rind—
a delicate strata of green between—

sit empty on the board, await
division into sickle moons
or a filling of nut and fruit—

some tight-skinned, crunchy contrast
to the soft density, the heavy-wet
sweetness curled into the bowl of a spoon.

Dreher Island Produce

Prosperity, SC

By Terresa Haskew

Sunday morning at the State-sanctioned vegetable shed, a Mastiff the size of a miniature donkey thumps his tail at your approach to a table laden with today's offerings—golden gourds of summer squash, green thumbs of cucumbers, perfect for pickling, and those tomatoes! Your hand hovers over ruby fruit on the verge of bursting with flavor. Lift the lids on hampers of hoed potatoes, small reds and whites dusty as the bare feet of farm children. Crates of Silver Queen corn stand open for close inspection. Your nail sinks easily into kernels clad in nature's silk.

No grocer's shelves for this harvest. No fluorescents or sprays of fake rain. Only the hot circle of the sun shines here, and the cool moon. No scanners or ringing registers, just the high whine of taste-testing yellow jackets and wind bending a cardboard sign outlining prices per pound. Bag and weigh your selections. Calculate the cost as dirt cheap, then multiply by two. Be generous. The big dog guards the bounty, ensures you brought your honor with the bills you slip into the slot of a locked metal box. You leave with a heavy haul, feeling like a thief stealing a sovereign's gold, for you know one can never pay enough for the treasures of this red earth's issue.

'Que

By Frank Thompson

Barbeque is, in my vocabulary, primarily a noun. Specifically, it is the smoked meat of a pig, cooked slowly over a hickory pit. It is steeped in lore and legend, with specific rituals and procedures. Regional variations abound, and there seems to be surprisingly little consensus over what stands out as the best style of cooking, sauce, and presentation. From the smoked beef ribs of Texas to the vinegar-and-pepper-sauce of an Outer Banks pig-pickin', loyalists stand behind their favorites, and I am no exception.

Coming from a distinguished line of Alabama grill men, (Dear Old Dad's sauce still being the rigid family standard by which all others wither), I am firmly loyal to the ketchup-based, brownish-red, Worcestershire-infused tangy sweetness upon which I was weaned. The zingy yellow mustard sauce of SC has taken a bit of getting used to, as it provides a sort of day-after-Easter ham sandwichy taste. Not quite BBQ, but enjoyable.

Knowing of my love for red BBQ sauce, a friend suggested that I try Little Pigs Barbeque here in Columbia. I was not disappointed. As a matter of fact, I kind of fell in love with it. I knew my primary gustatory needs of fried/ketchupy/salty/greasy would be satisfied as soon as I entered and smelled the specific aroma that only that particular amalgam can create. Little Pigs smells satisfying. It smells like beach food, like something served in either a shiny red or yellow plastic basket lined with a sheet of soon-to-be translucent waxy paper. It smells like the fair. It smells crunchy and brown and good.

I took perfunctory dollops of Cole slaw, baked beans and potato salad, basically as grace notes. A little pulled pork and a single rib joined them for the main event. Was it life-changing or even remotely Dear Old Dad's? No. Was it tasty, well-cooked and something I would happily eat again? Absolutely. Ironically, the one "Sweet Mother of God, this is good" moment came with the fried chicken, which blossoms crunchy, salty, soft and savory all at once.

What grabbed me about Little Pigs Barbeque was the potential for people-watching. I saw several overweight biker-types, with the almost courtly courtesy that bikers often have. It struck me as delightfully incongruous when the guy with ZZ Top hair and tattoos held out the chair for his elderly lunch companion (his mother perhaps) and took obvious care in her comfort and enjoyment of the day. Books and their covers, indeed.

I also saw a table full of young men, presumably construction workers or gardeners. They were sweaty and dirty, yet filled with a palpable optimism and good cheer. Four or five of them, early to mid-twenties, sat eating, talking, and laughing. The energy from their side of the room was glowing with youth and promise. These were puppies, their coats shiny, their energy boundless, and their lives ahead of them. I think I was their age yesterday.

There was the lipstick-and-heels girl whose click-clack staccato footsteps drew almost as much attention as her plunging scarlet neckline ... the young family ... the unkempt, mustached policeman (who was most likely having lunch with his wife, but whom I imagined to be meeting some sketchy sex worker with whom he was having a torrid pay-for-play affair) ... the random office workers and anonymous background players ... and then there was the MeeMaw table.

Seated in the center of the room were four women, each somewhere in her 60s or early 70s. One had a brown bouffant, one a sassy-old-lady shag, and the other two wore variations of both. The brown-bouffanted one had on a polyester pantsuit and wore her glasses, hand to God, on a chain around her neck. She was my own grandmother, circa 1981. They chatted and chuckled, occasionally allowing a word or two to waft free of their enclave.

"I declare ..."

"He ought to know better than that ..."

"Hon, come on over, we've got plenty ..."

"It was so hot the other day ..."

Now, these may have been the most erudite sophisticates within a hundred miles, worth millions each, but I instantly assigned them to a world of Friday visits to the beauty shop at Sears with coffee afterward, Baptist Church potluck suppers, funeral home fans on the front porch, and use of the terms "icebox" and "chifforobe" and the expression "Lord willing." Far from disliking these women, I felt a strange urge to join them, to ask them to insist that I eat more, that I look after myself, and to generally fuss and cluck over me. I wanted to feel the scratchy softness of a polyester jacket against the back of my forearm as I hugged them hello, and I wanted to smell the Jergens hand lotion and Rose Milk dusting powder. I wanted to hear the sweetly croaking voices offer unsolicited life advice. I wanted to politely ask if I could just sit with them and soak up their collective essence. I wanted to ask them to help me revisit my own childhood for a minute or two.

I didn't do that, of course. I finished eating and left, having sampled the bizarre but tasty dessert of chocolate pudding, peanut butter, vanilla wafers and whipped cream. It kind of makes the corners of your mouth ache, but in a good way. Trust me; it tastes better than it sounds. I hope the MeeMaws had some.

Independence Day

By Ed Madden

1.

Missed it again this year, the guns-n-God
pageant at First Baptist, armed guards

invading the aisles. They'll play it later on one
channel or another—they always do. At ten,

Juan and two men whose names we didn't
get were banging up sheetrock in the basement—

air conditioning claiming another room. *The Fourth's
not a holiday for them*, Juan says. Next door

a guy is singing, *Girl what you drinkin?
Go on let it sink in. Here for the weekend.*

By afternoon the men are slapping up mud
downstairs, slathering joints, hiding the studs

where we'd thought to write our names.

2.

The humidity has lifted a bit, the breeze still
wicked hot, even zinnias beginning to wilt

out front. This morning I watered the gerbers heavy,
clumps of leaves furled, curled up and ready

for the sun to smack them down hard, the way
it does. Our neighbor Ginger stopped by to say

hi, and eye up our new mailbox of rock, mortared
by a guy halfway home in the house next door.

Along the front walk, something's eating
the sunflowers, petals clipped, leaves bitten

to lace—bug-bit eclipse—and a green rash
of aphids like little blisters, swarms of ants

tending them, drawn to the sugary shit they secrete,
honeydew, sticky and sweet. They'll bite off the wings

to keep them put. We want what we want.

3.

Whitman walked the hospital wards on the Fourth,
1863, with bottles of cherry syrup,

stirred into ice water, dispensing sweet
drinks to the boys with news of the war, Meade's

victory, Lee's retreat—*good and strong*,
he wrote, *but innocent*—the bells ringing sundown

peals, the usual fusillades of crackers and guns.

4.

We heard firecrackers earlier, but now, the suburbs
at sundown, just the bravuras of birds,

and next door I hear America singing, *Blame it
on the ah-ah-ah-alcohol.* The mudmen are paid

and gone, the drywall done. Red buds
of montbretia in the bed near the road

pack stems like firecrackers' green wicks,
clusters seething and lit, the cleome's pink

waits in the heat, a dirty bomb of seed.

Worship at Lake Murray

By Terresa Haskew

Just before Black's Bridge
he brings the bow around,
steering starboard
in a graceful arc of spray,
shoreline trees sweeping
a cloudless sapphire sky.

In drowse of heat I lift my face
to firmament's call for offerings,
salute the sun with a Solo cup
of Bloody Mary steadied
through swells and swales of wake,
morning's moon a pale crescent nail
of our Maker's hand twirling his re-creation.
Praise for the sunshine! Praise for vacation!
Ours is the morning, ours the whole day.

Forbidden Fruit

By Melissa Johnson

makes jam
the rural church sign
—weed surrounded—read.

Puzzled, pricked,
we begged to differ—
jam is sweet

essential fruit
glistening jewel-like
piquant with pectin

scooped and spread
to gild crisp toast,
licked from a finger,

offered like myrrh
in pretty pots—
unending harvest,

weedless, seedless,
without blisters,
temperate and pest-free,

Like all sin,
easy to take up,
hard to shake off.

Smell

Chinese Snowball Viburnum
at Riverbanks Botanical Gardens
By Melissa Johnson

Globes of floating luminosity
like Parrish's lanterns;
hundreds of white balloons,
all light and lift, weightless.

Cupped in a palm,
they are pendulous,
more ivory than snowy,
lace of myriad five-petalled stars,
a chartreuse dot at each center.
Lifted not by lantern bearers
but hanging from branches,
a shrub posing as tree,
trunk divided, fullness illusory.

Not light, not tree, not floating,
far from cold and snow,
the other side of the earth from China,
smelling not of candleflame,
nor of winter crisp, but faintly
of rain washed lilac, the tang
of rot and cat underneath.

I bury my face again and again
in illusion, the faint whiff of decay.

As I Look Back

By Mahayla Bainter

The smell of sweaty bodies slammed together hit me. Everybody sweated on the bus. We were in a hunk of metal that got too hot or way too cold. There was no in between. It was a frosty mobile or a burning machine of death. It got us to and from school.

I loved it, though, because I could sit and chat with whoever was on the bus. The taste of electric hate and hormones all crammed together. The sight of people leaning over seats to get the latest gossip. The sound of it as I sat quiet and tried to overhear without being noticed. The cracked red-brown seats made sounds of farts that everyone laughed at. The overly dressed with the underdressed, it was a crazy mixture of colors the eyes couldn't keep up with. They all moved around too fast.

If you were the unlucky one, they would get together and pick on you. It was a crazy mix that couldn't be tamed. We were young and uncaring. We truly had no worries.

Now I just look back and remember how it was. How I wish it could be again. Just to go back and smell the heavy electricity and anticipation of rain. I always wanted freedom. Now I realize that back then I had the freedom even if I didn't know it. The sound of uncaring laughter and the feel of the deep belly laugh. To be there again and to be young.

Your confession on the pontoon near Jake's Landing

By Linda Lee Harper

We shouldn't tell each other secrets.
They molder under our tongues.

They have a need to spill out like maggots exposed.
They never respect their elders.

They almost always smell like whatever died under the porch.
In sunlight, they appear ephemeral, almost irrelevant.

At night, they own the room, the bed, your head.
When it's time to acknowledge them, they lie, deny knowing you.

And when you finally admit there may be some truth to them,
they slink away, softly subversive as a fleshy nude

painted on a church's basement wall.

When Dawn Comes

By Cassie Premo Steele

We don't talk about it much, but it's common: a writer spends years working on a book, gets ready to submit it for publication, and after nine months or two years or a decade of rejections, gives up.

The writer hides it in a file in her computer and tries to forget that it – and the memory of the rejections – are there. Sometimes, in the olden days of years ago, a writer would print it out — just in case the computer crashed – and put it in an attic or a closet.

I've done this, too. I've put novels under my bed. My marriage bed.

They stayed there, gathering dust, for years.

The irony is that the one I had the hardest time with was a novel about marriage. I'd never quite poured so much of myself into fiction before. During part of the novel, when the main character's husband is in the hospital, my husband was, too.

Fiction is like this. It has a spooky, uncanny way of creating reality. Long ago, just starting out, I was writing a scene in a novel about a bored and retired grandfather, driving in long, slow arcs around his neighborhood in his white Cadillac to kill time. And I looked up to find an older man driving his white Cadillac in a loop around our cul de sac.

I got a little afraid of fiction. It was this spookiness, and the fact that the agent who read that novel said, "I do not love this at all."

One agent. One rejection. And I gave up on fiction. This, dear reader, is called inexperience.

I soon became experienced.

The next novel I wrote was at first a memoir about my family's relationship with Ireland as the motherland. That same agent – she had stayed with me after that first disaster – gave the second book a read. This, dear reader, is called fucking fantastic luck.

She didn't like that one, either, though. "There's not enough of *you* in it," she said. "Or there's too much of you and not enough of a *story*."

I had no idea what she meant.

But I was determined to learn. I turned that personal memoir about my family into a novel about globalization that flung characters all over the world. I was starting to get what the agent had meant about good writing—the triangulated paradox of me/not me/story.

The spookiness happened again while writing this novel. I created a character from India who struggled with his mixed Muslim-Hindu heritage. Before I knew it, I was sitting next to a man who could have been this character at a banquet for a literary conference my husband was leading. And before we knew it, I was in that man's hotel room.

There was much talk and a kiss, but the main thing that lingers with me is the blue dawn light surrounding me driving home.

It's my favorite time of day to write. I love the way I glow in front of the computer screen and a candle in the dark before dawn, as my tea sits cold next to me and the words spill out like the sun coming up.

That moment when you realize the light is in your room, between your hands and your face and the screen and all around your body—it's as if you somehow participated in the coming of this light through your writing.

That morning, driving home, I realized that this sunrise time after an encounter with someone who felt like a creation from your own writing is, for a writer, very close to writing.

It's a sacred time. And *sacred* is connected to *scared* like a metaphor is connected to our hearts when we read a poem.

So my marriage survived all that. And I ended up publishing that novel, which is called *Shamrock and Lotus*. So my writing survived, too.

And I kept writing. Since writing *Shamrock and Lotus*, I've published four poetry books and three more nonfiction books (I already had two under my belt) and co-created two musical poetry albums.

I also wrote two more novels. One is about American history, and one is about marriage and war.

This second one has that me/not me/story triangle to it: it is the story of an American military wife whose husband is wounded during his third tour in Afghanistan. Three kids, three deployments. I wanted to witness to this. I felt I could, actually, because of the fact that it *wasn't* my story.

So I wrote intensely during a summer when my husband was hospitalized three times. The husband in the novel was in a hospital at Landstuhl in Germany, and the wife character flies to see him. My husband had just been released from the hospital when I flew to Miami to witness the birth of my sister's daughter. My husband was supposed to travel to Turkey for a conference. I convinced him not to go. Planes and hospitals and the fear of losing a husband in a hospital or a foreign country fueled the writing of the novel.

I had admitted to myself earlier that I was treading dangerous territory when I wrote fiction. Was it the weaving of my obsession with traumatic histories that brought this upon me? Or was I some kind of witch when I wrote, interrupting the cosmic warp and creating a new reality?

The worst day was this: I finished my pre-dawn and early morning writing outside, and the air was not yet too hot, so I decided to cut the grass.

The whir of the lawn mower's engine and the vibration in my hands and the great humidity brewing in the air and my own sweat in my eyes brought the feeling of combat into my body, and suddenly I was my character, the soldier husband, on a hot mountain.

The next thing I knew, the motor let out a deafening metallic boom and pieces flew into my eyes and onto my skin. And then there was deafening silence. And blood.

I leaned down, and there, still alive, was an Eastern box turtle with its shell blown off by the blades of the mower. The shell was still pooling with blood from capillaries cut at odd angles, and the flesh was still a warm yellowish pink.

I knew this turtle. We called him Martin Luther King, Jr. He lived in the creek behind our house and visited occasionally. As a result, he was both a member of our family and a foreigner. I'd written essays about him. My daughter would be devastated.

I kneeled down and prayed for forgiveness. He died as

I prayed. I took what was left of the body and buried it under the cedar trees.

I finished mowing the lawn. I, like a soldier, had a job to do.

Then I went up to our bedroom where the previous novels had hidden under our bed, and I took off my flesh-splattered clothes. I was shaking. I put them in the wash, realizing too late that I should have taken them off outside and thrown them out right away.

That dusty pink wife beater t-shirt went in with the rest of the family's laundry that week, and then for months it lingered in the bottom of a drawer, where I lost my breath whenever I saw it. Until one day I finally threw it out. Its ghost still lives in that drawer.

I didn't tell my daughter what I'd done. I couldn't. I told my husband, and as usual, when faced with death, he responded with disbelief and then blame.

It's not as if I didn't deserve the blame. I was the killer, after all.

I poured all of this out of me in the coming mornings at dawn as the soldier husband kills his team's Afghani translator by mistake on a raid.

This was something bigger than the old man driving around the cul de sac. This was even bigger than a kiss in a hotel room with another man.

This was war.

And I felt it in me. The terror underneath the skin, like someone places a needle there and forgets to take it out. The way the muscles converge around the pain and begin to harden and become the pain itself.

The way the pain goes away with pills and drinking.

Until it doesn't.

I had such pain. It began at the base of my spine when I finished writing the novel and over the next nine months, it spread throughout my spine and into my head until eventually I had a mini-stroke in the right somatosensory cortex of my brain— the area that controls feeling.

The doctors found no cause.

But I felt cursed.

I have a writer friend whose parents are from India, and I was talking to her over a year after writing the novel, and months after the stroke, telling her how I'd received rejection after rejection for the book.

She reminded me of the turtle. "Trauma is contagious," she said.

As she spoke, three hawks circled overhead near our creek. The hawks are my writing companions. They come, often, when I am on the wrong path, or want to be on a different path, or when I am confused, or need guidance.

"I'll let the novel go," I said. "It's infected me. I can't witness to these wars. It's not my story."

It wasn't my war.

This wasn't my book.

Fast-forward six months. I've started singing versions of my poems with a woman musician, and we go to a gig out of town. On the way home, she asks me about the novel. She is the editor of the newspaper at Fort Jackson, the nearby army post. She is interested.

I tell her as much as I can about the story of writing the novel. I don't mention the turtle, though. The story of the turtle is sacred to me. Deeper than poetry and song.

She listens, and then she says, "There's a woman here who's helping the Army wives with writing classes. Maybe she would be interested in what you do."

Something opened in me. Maybe all of this – the novel, my writing, my pain — could be put to some use. It was like the first hint of light long before the dawn.

I met with the woman who ran the writing group for wives, and we were like soul mates.

"I never meant to marry a soldier," she said. "I married a man, and then 9/11 happened."

I knew what she meant. I never meant to write that novel. For both of us, love came first – her love for her husband, my love for the me/not me/story of fiction writing – and then there we were.

She invited me to give a workshop on writing as a way of healing for her group. I said yes.

As the date drew near, I felt scared again. How could I help these women? I knew nothing. Nothing.

A few nights before the workshop, I had a dream that I met a family along a river. The husband told me he'd been deployed three times, and as his wife and son and daughter looked on, I said to him, "I wrote a novel about that."

The dream then skips to the middle of the night. The phone rings. I pick it up. It is the wife. Her husband, she tells me, has just hung himself. She asks if she and her children can come down the river so I can help them. I say yes.

I wake.

I felt I'd caused his suicide. By my pride. By trying to write something I knew nothing about.

I emailed my sound healer – a woman with one name who lives in California and creates sound healing meditations I listen to every weekday morning. She had really helped me before, during, and after the chronic pain and stroke. I asked her about the dream.

Her one-word answer: Compassion.

Yes. Okay, I breathed. That's what I needed. That's all I needed to stand in the place where I am and yet write about people who don't exist. And yet who do.

The night I drove to Fort Jackson for the workshop, I had the same feeling I had the first time I visited Germany. Years of Holocaust literature had made me fear Nazis everywhere I turned. The memories were still there. The same cities. The same language. The same buildings.

Someone who was just going there for the first time would feel it in a way that someone whose blood inhaled it from birth would not. I felt the fear, and the denial, and the violence, and the secrecy – and yet these were just words. What I really felt was a great pain. And a pain that the people themselves could not ever really pull themselves away from without help from someone outside the borders.

I handed my license to the guard at the gate and part of me wanted to blurt out, "I'll pull the blanket off all of this! Don't let me in!"

I stayed quiet.

The workshop went well. As it always does, writing led

us. We sat in a room in a circle and I read my poems – about marriage, about mothering, about loss and separation and reunion – to them, and some of them cried, and we meditated and wrote and talked together. The work was done in the space we shared between our differences.

After the workshop, one woman emailed me and asked to meet again. She didn't want to be my client. She wanted to be my friend. I already felt like I was becoming friends with the workshop leader, so I suggested we form a writing group. I needed one. It was time for me to admit what I needed.

As I write this, I am sitting by a pond at Fort Jackson on a beautiful day just before the spring equinox, and occasionally I can smell smoke from the weapons in the training grounds behind me. It smells like the motor of the lawn mower just after the blades stopped. It smells like acid. It smells like memories that people are making right now somewhere very far away.

It was that woman musician who brought me here. We met for lunch by the lake one day, and it was the nature that drew me in. A couple of ducks. Spanish moss in the trees. Loblollies.

Like the wife of the soldier in my novel, I live only a few miles away from here. But I've never been here, not with someone from here.

Because after I met her at work and as she drove me to the lake where she sits alone some days at lunch to rest from being surrounded by men and military code, she described what we were seeing.

"Our PX. Our officers' quarters. Our new residences."

It was the *our* that drew me in.

Because we had used this word for our poemsongs, too. My words, her music – and yet, with trust, we come together to co-create something else and new. Something that is ours.

She is from Germany. And suddenly next to that lake, I was in the mountains circling the German town of Heidelberg, where she went to school and where I felt for the first time in Germany, not the ghosts of the Holocaust, but the legacies of the philosophers and the deep regard for nature in the work of German theologians and philosophers that runs like a river through the center of the city.

I stayed up all night in Heidelberg, I remembered. I was there in June and the university students had just finished their exams and the streets were brimming with laughter and beer and the late night sun of Europe's summer.

I stayed up all night with the musician after one of our gigs, too. We talked and listened to music and felt what we were creating through the open circle of the shared space of our difference. As the first blue light of dawn came through the windows, I said, "Let's go watch."

And we were in suburb of a mid-size southern city, just like the best friend of the wife of the soldier in the novel. And once again what I'd written on the page felt like it was foretelling what was happening in my life. As if time and space in the creative universe indeed moves back and forth like scientists are starting to understand.

"Dawn is my favorite time of day," I told her.

"Me, too," she said.

"I write then," I said.

And then a song came on her computer's iTunes shuffle:

> This is the greatest time of day
> when all the clocks are spinning backwards
> and all the ropes that bind begin to fray
> and all the black and white turns into
> colors.

"What is this song?" I asked her.

She told me.

"What are the chances of this song playing at the exact moment of dawn?"

"I have no idea," she said. "I have about fourteen days worth of songs on that computer."

And in that moment it was as if the nighttime trajectory of destruction that was put into motion when I wrote that novel and that bound me to war and the turtle and his death and my pain and my fear and the stroke – all this started moving forward into the light again.

Between the Army and me.

Between Germany and me.

Between marriage and loss.

Between writing and killing.

Between the philosophers and the forest.

Between the hawk and the turtle.

When dawn comes, it is my favorite time of day. I love the way I write in the glow from my computer screen and a candle in the dark before dawn, as my tea sits cold next to me and the words spill out like the sun coming up.

I love that moment when you realize the light is in your room, between your hands and your face and the screen and all around your body, as it's as if you somehow participated in this coming light through your writing.

And I love the way you can return to that moment of dawn through writing – not just when you write, but when you wait, and you heal and you grow and you persist and you revise and you try again.

I've done a few writing workshops for military women at Fort Jackson now, and I've become part of the writing group that was born the night of that first workshop, and I've had some of the military wives read my novel and respond with heartfelt enthusiasm and support. I am ready now, to find an agent who loves this book and understands the sacred power that writing holds for our healing.

Right now, by the lake at Fort Jackson, it is possible still to smell the smoke from gunfire and watch two ducks in formation and see vultures and hawks circling. These things survive – just as we survive – as long as we are alive to keep writing.

Anytime writing connects us to the pain of the past and circles into the present and provides a light for the future, it's a sacred time.

And while I used to think that sacred is connected to scared like a metaphor is connected to our hearts when we read in a poem, I no longer think that.

Because I've gotten support from other women and I've come to claim my full self as a writer and a woman. And I'm not scared.

Salt Atlas

By Matthew Fogarty

Train Yard

I leap off the overpass onto a hurtling freight and ride it to the other coast, dive off the pier and swim the ocean, spray up out of the Pacific at some point, a bursting explosion of salt water, shooting up like a rocket, flying fist-forward through the atmosphere into space. My knuckle cracks the jaw of the moon.

Greenway

We followed the path through the park and into that tunnel where the trains used to run—the city above, the echo, the stone gray walls, the blacktop pathway where the rails were, and us: cells in a big gray vein.

Pearls

I saw a kid slice through his hand one night at the Oyster Bar and it kind of set a bad tone. I was on a date with a woman I'd met online. Her profile said she was adventurous and liked seafood and I'm adventurous and like seafood and so I sent her a message even though we were only a fifty-nine percent match. I decided to be a little more forward than usual: *Do you believe in soulmates?* I asked. *Based on your profile, I believe you could be mine.*

She replied within an hour: *Sure, what the hell. Let's get oysters.*

Oysters. The ultimate aphrodisiac. We ordered two dozen.

I was in my seersucker; she was in a bright orange dress.

Her laugh was more like a crow's *caw* than anything human. Her lipstick was crooked and her teeth were too white. She smelled of the sea. But I was sure she had a good heart.

And there, too, was the college kid on the other side of the metal bar. He brought out a bucketful from the back, threw a white towel over his shoulder, and started jabbing his knife into the shells and pounding them on a wood block. I could tell he was new: his hands were shaky and his grip kept slipping—first the oyster shell, then the knife handle, too. Nor did he throw out any witty banter like the other shuckers.

Not that we paid much attention. We were engaged in that typical first date *tet-a-tet*. She used all her body to flirt, especially her legs, and the conversation was thick and layered. We disagreed about the meanings of things—religious signs and sacrifices, foreign aid, the confederate flag. Part of me wanted to fast-forward to an anniversary, years from now, when we'd look back on this awkward time as the start of our complex and dynamic relationship. I was tired of dating, tired of eating alone. Supermarkets don't sell bachelor portions.

And that's when it happened. I turned toward the kid just as the shell slipped and the knife caromed off it and into the flesh of the kid's palm. He let out a coarse shriek. It was the first time I'd seen a tendon, though I didn't get a great look before the whole hand spilled over with blood.

The other guys were johnnies-on-the-spot with it, and they had towels out and were all apologetic even before most of the other people at the bar fully realized what had happened.

They got the kid off to the hospital and we were both a

little traumatized and we'd kind of lost our appetites so we decided to end the date there. Except that, on our way out, she turned back to the manager, who still had a starfish splatter of blood on his shirt, and she asked if she could have a bag of discarded shells. I thought for a moment there was hope; I formed this romantic image in my mind of her making some sort of macramé art or creating an oyster garden off of which the sun would glint at just the right angle, cast a ray through her kitchen window, light her from just the right angle to highlight her true goodness inside. With a smear of something red below her lip (blood maybe or cocktail sauce), she turned back to me and said, *I just like them for the smell—the smell of old seafood.*

I never saw her again.

Quarry

That summer when everything was idle I would sneak past the gate to the quarry and run down the path to the bottom of it, to the center, and look up at the tall round gunpowder walls, concentric like the place had been cleared out by an auger or cratered by a collision with the moon, like it was a cast of the moon. I heard once that in the 70s they used the quarry to practice for one of the moon landings, that they shipped the rover and the equipment and the space suits and the astronauts up here one summer and they drove around the stones and the pits of the quarry floor and stuck a flag in the middle of it. And I realize it's probably not true. Things you hear once are almost never true and I don't even know if the quarry was around back then. But if I were running the space program I'd have done it—it would have made sense. Not because of the steep rock walls or the depth of the crater or the way in which the quarry floor looks just like the moon's surface. But because of the desolation, the uniform black gray of it, the loneliness. It just seems to me that the big challenge of the moonshot—all of the science and other technical stuff aside—is that when you're on the moon you're so far away from home and you're alone and you can't breathe at all and all you've got to protect you is this thin tinfoil ship and all you can think after coming so far is how to get back to where you started, back out of the quarry and out onto the other side of the gate toward home.

About the Writers

Lauren Allen grew up in Kershaw County and is currently earning her MFA in Creative Nonfiction at the University of South Carolina. She won the 2011 South Carolina Writers Workshop annual Carrie McCray Awards for Nonfiction and for Poetry and recently her poem "corduroy road" was nominated by *The Petigru Review* for a 2014 Pushcart Prize.

Nan Ancrom is a recipient of the South Carolina Arts Commission poetry fellowship. Her poems have appeared in *The Nation*, *Rolling Stone*, and many journals and magazines.

Mahayla Bainter is a 17-year-old freshman in college who loves to read and write stories. She plans to become a lawyer.

James Barilla is the author of books and articles about the human relationship with the natural world. He teaches creative nonfiction in the MFA program at the University of South Carolina.

Jennifer Bartell is pursuing an MFA in Creative Writing from the University of South Carolina and is an alumna of Agnes Scott College. Her poetry has been published in *Jasper Magazine*, *The Art of Medicine in Metaphors* anthology, and *Letras Caseras*. She is the the poetry editor of *Yemassee*, USC's literary journal.

Julie E. Bloemeke's poems have most recently appeared in *A&U: America's AIDS Magazine*, *Qarrtsiluni*, and in the collaborative chapbook *Jasper Reads: Download*. In spring, 2012, her series of poetry and photography on abandoned spaces was featured in *Deep South Magazine*. Her poetry and non-fiction are forthcoming in a number of anthologies including *The Southern Poetry Anthology Volume V: Georgia*

Laurel Blossom is the author of *Degrees of Latitude*, a book-length narrative poem published in 2007, as well as *Wednesday: New and Selected Poems*, *The Papers Said*, *What's Wrong*, and *Any Minute*. Her sixth book, *Longevity*, will be published in 2015.

Matthew Boedy is a PhD candidate in rhetoric at the University of South Carolina and has published short stories in several online journals. He has an MFA from USC, as well.

Cynthia Boiter is the author of *Buttered Biscuits: Short Stories from the South*, the co-author of *Red Social: Portraits of Collaboration*, the editor of *The Limelight: A Compendium of Contemporary Columbia Artists*, and the editor-in-chief of *Jasper Magazine – The Word on Columbia Arts*.

Darien Cavanaugh received his MFA from the University of South Carolina. His work has been published or is forthcoming in *The Dos Passos Review*, *Memoir* (and), *The Blue Collar Review*, *The Coe Review*, *Struggle*, *Pank*, *The Blue Earth Review*, *The James Dickey Newsletter*, *Gertrude*, *I-70 Review*, *Rolling Thunder Quarterly*, *Kakalak*, *Burningword*, and *The San Pedro River Review*. He lives in Columbia, SC, and works at The Whig.

Matthew Fogarty was born in Detroit but currently lives in Columbia where he is an MFA candidate at the University of South Carolina. An alum of the Squaw Valley Community of Writers, his fiction has appeared or is forthcoming in *Revolution House*, *Umbrella Factory*, *Midwestern Gothic*, and *Zero Ducats*.

Melanie Griffin came to the Midlands for college and has been here ever since. She works in Human Resources at the Richland Library and has been published in *Alligator Juniper* and *robocup press* (photos).

Linda Lee Harper has published seven chapbooks, including *Blue Flute* and received three Yaddo fellowships, four Pushcart nominations, and been published in over a hundred literary journals including *The Georgia Review, Nimrod, Beloit Poetry Journal, Rattle, Southern Poetry Review*, and others.

Kristine Hartvigsen is the author of *To the Wren Nesting*, a book of poetry, and associate editor of *Jasper Magazine – The Word on Columbia Arts*.

Terresa Haskew's work won the *Emrys Journal* 2013 Nancy Dew Taylor Poetry Award and the *Press 53* 2010 First Prize for Poetry. Her poetry chapbook *Breaking Commandments* is available through Main Street Rag Publishing Company. Terresa's poems and stories have also appeared in journals such as *Atlanta Review, Jasper, moonShine Review* and *Pearl*.

Melissa Johnson's poetry has appeared in *Borderlands, Waccamaw, Kakalak, The Connecticut Review, Farmer's Market, The Potomac Review,* and *The Cortland Review*. Her chapbook, *Looking Twice at the World*, was a winner of the 2007 South Carolina Poetry Initiative Chapbook Contest.

Ed Madden is an associate professor of English at USC and author of three books of poetry: *Signals, Prodigal: Variation,* and *Nest*. He is also literary arts editor *for Jasper Magazine – The Word on Columbia Arts.*

Thomas Maluck earned a BA in English and philosophy as well as a Masters in Library and Information Science from the University of South Carolina. His poems have appeared in chapbooks published by Stepping Stone Press and the

South Carolina Arts Institute.

Ray McManus is the author of three books of poetry: *Red Dirt Jesus*, *Left Behind*, and *Driving through the country before you are born*. His poetry has appeared most recently in *Blue Collar Review*, *Barely South*, *The Pinch*, *Hayden's Ferry*, and *moonShine Review*.

Rieppe Moore's poetry collections include *Actual Seconds*, *Letters to Ethiopia* and a chapbook, *Windows Behind the Veil*. While in his first year teaching English, he began writing his second chapbook to be published later this year.

Zach Mueller graduated from the University of South Carolina's MFA program in 2012. His poems are in *Gulf Coast, Prairie Schooner, Rattle, Heavy Feather Review*, and other places. He currently teaches creative writing at Franklin College in Indiana and is from Blythewood, South Carolina.

Brandi L. Perry is a student in the MFA program in Creative Writing at the University of South Carolina. A James Dickey Fellow and inaugural SPARC Fellowship awardee she is the co-editor of *Yemassee* and *The Art of Medicine in Metaphors: A Collection of Poems and Narratives* (2013).

Tom Poland is the author of six books and more than 800 magazine features. The University of South Carolina Press released his latest book, *Save The Last Dance For Me* in 2012 and will publish *Reflections of South Carolina*, Vol. II, in the spring of 2014 and later *Georgialina, A Southland*.

Robbie Pruitt is a poet from South Carolina who currently lives in Haiti. A graduate of Columbia International University in Columbia, SC, he enjoys writing poetry and blogging about leadership and theology.

Dianne Turgeon Richardson is a native South Carolinian

and MFA candidate at the University of Central Florida, where she is a managing editor of *The Florida Review*. Her work has appeared in *The Holler Box, Zaum 17, Blue Fish Digest,* and *Gently Read Literature*.

Kevin Simmonds' books include *Mad for Meat, Ota Benga Under My Mother's Roof,* and *Collective Brightness: LGBTIQ Poets on Faith, Religion & Spirituality*. He wrote the music for the Emmy Award-winning documentary *HOPE: Living and Loving with HIV in Jamaica* and, most recently, *Voices from Haiti*, both commissioned by the Pulitzer Center.

Randolph Spencer is a physician and poet living in Chapin, South Carolina. He received his MFA in Poetry from the University of South Carolina in 2002. He has published two chapbooks of poetry, *The Failure of Magic* and, most recently, *What the Body Knows*, published through the South Carolina Poetry Initiative in 2010.

Cassie Premo Steele, Ph.D., is a writing coach and the author of 12 books of poetry, fiction, and non-fiction. Her poetry has been nominated three times for the Pushcart Prize, and she writes a column for *Literary Mama* and blogs for the *Huffington Post*.

Alexis Stratton received an MFA in Creative Writing from the University of South Carolina. Her fiction has recently appeared in *Ayris Magazine, Breakwater Review,* and *Bare Root Review*, and she won the 2012 BLOOM Chapbook Contest for Fiction.

Frank Thompson is a graduate of The University of Alabama and Cumberland School of Law. He has written several unpublished-but-performed scripts for local theatre companies and is currently working on a history of Alice, the resident ghost at Columbia's Town Theatre.

Ruth Varner won First Place in the Amateur Short Story Competition in *Lake Murray Magazine* and was recently published in *The Art of Medicine in Metaphors, A Collection of Poems and Narratives.*

Nicola Waldron is the recipient of the United Kingdom's Bridport Poetry Prize and has had recent poems and essays featured in *Borderlands: Texas Poetry Review*, *Free State Review*, *The Common*, *Places Journal* and *Her Kind*. Her chapbook *Girl at the Watershed* was chosen for publication through the University of South Carolina's Poetry Initiative.

P. Ivan Young is author of *A Shape in the Waves* and the 2013 winner of the Norton Girault Literary Prize. His most recent publications are in *Myrrh, Mothwig, Smoke: Erotic Poems* and in *Hayden's Ferry Review, Fourteen Hills, Zone 3, The Cortland Review,* and *Crab Orchard Review.*

About the Cover Artist

Jarid Lyfe Brown was born in 1974 in Atlanta, Georgia and moved to South Carolina in 1980. He studied painting at The Savannah College of Art and Design in Savannah, Georgia and has been painting for over 20 years. Brown creates anthropomorphic figures in atmospheres of literature, life experiences, and various emotions using painting, drawing, and writing. Brown wants private and intimate moments to be presented as honest and straightforwardly as possible. He is influenced by life, family, current events, other local and international artists, street art, and graffiti. Jarid Lyfe Brown lives and paints in South Carolina with his wife, one son, and two daughters.

About the Publisher

Muddy Ford Press, LLC is a boutique publishing company dedicated to providing hands-on juried publishing opportunities to writers and poets from South Carolina and beyond.

Find us at MuddyFordPress.com.

Also from Muddy Ford Press

Jasper Reads: Download
edited by Ed Madden

To the Wren Nesting
by Kristine Hartvigsen

Buttered Biscuits: Short Stories from the South
by Cynthia Boiter

Fellow Traveler
by James D. McCallister

The Limelight, volume I
edited by Cynthia Boiter

All the In Between: My Story of Agnes
by Laurie McIntosh

Red Social: Portraits of Collaboration
by Alejandro Garcia-Lemos and Cynthia Boiter

Jasper Presents The 2nd Act Film Festival Screenplays
edited by Wade Sellers and Cynthia Boiter

Woman Commits Suicide in Dishwasher
by Debra A. Daniel

CPSIA information can be obtained at www.ICGtesting.com
Printed in the USA
LVOW06s1543090915

453467LV00017B/1048/P